'To see revival break ou[...]
God-given destiny. Mat[...]
on the 'destiny lifestyle'[...]
Gerald Coates, Team Lea[...]

'I have known Matt Bird [...] he worked with us as a student intern. He has integrity, passion for Christ and a deep desire to serve others. This book is, in part, a journal of his journey as a disciple – and I believe it will help others to find their place in God's purposes.'
Ian Coffey, Senior Minister, City Baptist Church, Plymouth

'There are many individuals who are currently concerned about the need to mentor younger men and women. Matt, who carries a passion for this important issue, is to be commended highly for committing himself and his ministry to this important task.'
Joel Edwards, General Director, Evangelical Alliance UK

'This book imparts a vision and passion for the purposes of God. Those who read it will be both stirred and also given practical input and direction concerning how to discover and pursue the purposes of God for their life. It is well worth a read.'
Roger Ellis, Leader, Revelation Church, Chichester

'Matt's easy and entertaining book deceptively hides the difficult, fresh, radical, pioneering ideas for the Twenty-First Century Christian until it's too late and you have swallowed the pill of challenge. A good read for aspiring servants of Christ. Beter still, do it!'
Roger and Faith Forster, Leaders, Ichthus Christian Fellowship

'Matt Bird's conviction that Christians can and do serve God in their daily lives – in the bar, the boardroom, the home and the shopfloor – is a message Christians have to take seriously if we are to reach the "unchurched" with the Gospel in the next millennium. A compelling book which all who seek to serve Christ in their daily lives should read.'
Jill Garrett, Managing Director, Gallup UK

'Matt Bird is committed to equipping today's Joshuas – to lead today's generation faced with all of today's moral and social problems.'
J. John, Director, Philo Trust

'The need to encourage and envision young adults has never been greater . . . I wholeheartedly endorse the work of Matt Bird.'
Sandy Millar, Vicar, Holy Trinity Brompton

'Matt Bird's radical message will inspire you to seize the day and fulfil your calling for the twenty-first century.'
Mike Pilavachi, Director, Soul Survivor

'We are all on a journey where the past becomes history, the future becomes a mystery and the present is a gift. Matt Bird's first book, *Destiny*, pulls no punches about leadership styles by tackling present issues to give tremendous hope for the rising generations of tomorrow.'
John S. Richardson, Provost, Bradford Cathedral

'Matt, a man on a unique personal journey, challenges his generation to find the true purpose of their lives.'
David Shearman, Senior Minister, Christian Centre Nottingham

'Matt Bird combines personal anecdotes, biblical knowledge and wise insights that come together in a delightful way. This is an excellent book that will help many young people as they seek to discover God's calling and direction for their lives. I thoroughly recommend it.'
Gary Streeter, MP for South West Devon

'Matt has written a helpful book for those who dream of being on the cast of *Friends* but know there is something far greater to discover and be.'
Phil Wall, National Evangelist, Salvation Army

Destiny

Discover the Life you were Created to Live

Matt Bird

with Craig Borlase

Hodder & Stoughton

LONDON SYDNEY AUCKLAND

Unless otherwise indicated, Scripture quotations are taken from the HOLY BIBLE, NEW INTERNATIONAL VERSION. Copyright © 1973, 1978, 1984 by International Bible Society. Used by permission. All rights reserved.

Copyright © 2000 by Matt Bird and Craig Borlase

First published in Great Britain in 2000

The right of Matt Bird and Craig Borlase to be identified as the Authors of the Work has been asserted by them in accordance with the Copyright, Designs and Patents Act 1988.

10 9 8 7 6 5 4 3 2

British Library Cataloguing in Publication Data
A record for this book is available from the British Library

ISBN 0 340 75616 0

Typeset by Avon Dataset Ltd, Bidford-on-Avon, Warks

Printed and bound in Great Britain by
The Guernsey Press Co. Ltd, Channel Isles

Hodder & Stoughton
A Division of Hodder Headline Ltd
338 Euston Road
London NW1 3BH

Contents

	Foreword	vii
	Thanks	ix
	Introduction	1
1	The Journeyer	5
2	The Lover	29
3	The Authenticator	49
4	The Innovator	75
5	The Empowerer	99
6	The Builder	119
7	The Relater	137
	Conclusion	155

Foreword

Mike Pilavachi

There are two urgent needs in the Church today; to make disciples and develop leaders. The Church's future is largely dependent on our getting these two things right. So many today are being filled, renewed and blessed, yet the Church of Jesus Christ in the United Kingdom is still shrinking. It is therefore more urgent than ever that we fulfil Jesus' mandate to make disciples of new believers, and help each one of them to live out their individual calling.

One of the keys that will unlock the door to revival is a generation of people who display their commitment to Christ in every aspect of their daily lives. The last thing we need is another generation of pew-warmers who don't know how to connect passion for Christ with living in the world. This book is a discipleship manual of tremendous importance. Matt Bird speaks to today's young Christians in their own language about the issues that are most relevant to them. *Destiny* connects faith and calling with living and working in the real world.

Matt convincingly explains how we must see our work and our whole life in the world as a calling and a vocation. Too many of us miss our destiny because we wait for it to fall out of the sky instead of realising that it is already here, just waiting for us to grasp it. True disciples of Jesus live as people of destiny because they discern their calling in the place and circumstances in which God has put them. They don't see working for the Church as the only – or even the most important – calling but instead take seriously Jesus' command to 'Go out into all the world'. Accountancy can be as much of a mission field as pastoring; working for Sainsbury's is as much a vocation as working for the Church Pastoral Aid Society.

Matt communicates these things both intelligently and passionately. His theology is well worked through and he's thrown in some great sound-bites that stick in the memory and help bring the message on home. No doubt they will become original Pilavachis in the years to come!

This is a book on leadership: about the need to raise up effective, Christian leaders in our world today. We need more of them serving in the Church – that's for sure – but we also need them to be the Church in the world. I have seen a generation of young Christians emerging in the last few years who want to change their world and are willing to pay the price in order to do so. If you are one of those people and you are longing to understand your destiny and to find the right tools to live it out, then this book is for you. The Joshua Generation conferences that Matt leads have helped many; it is timely that he has put down on paper some of the helpful and inspiring teaching from those conferences for a wider audience.

Mike Pilavachi
Soul Survivor

Thanks

To my prayer partners – Paul Lambert and Giles Mahoney – for being such good friends.

To the JoshGen: core team – Matt Stuart and Mary Johnson, trustees – David Curtis, Paul L and Paul Williams, and all you friends who stand with us.

To everyone at my church Pioneer People for being such a great home and family, and especially to Steve Clifford.

To friends who read and so helpfully commented on the manuscript of this book – Laurence Singlehurst, Simon Downham, Duncan Banks, Fiona McCurdy and Tim Coope.

To Craig Borlase for helping me to find the words to express what is on my heart, and to David Moloney, my editor, for liking the first idea, which his wise advice has shaped into something altogether better.

To the many people who have inspired and mentored me in pursuing my destiny, you know who you are.

Introduction

You're holding this book because I believe that we were born to lead. Let me explain. The Bible kicks off with a story of how God first chatted with Adam and Eve. 'God blessed them and said to them, "Be fruitful and increase in number; fill the earth and subdue it. Rule over the fish of the sea and the birds of the air and over every living creature that moves on the ground" ' (Genesis 1:28). Depending on your translation, we were designed and created to rule, steward or manage the Earth. Whatever you opt for, it's clear that we are here to make a difference and grab the wheel.

A bishop friend of mine talks about three sorts of leaders. First, that minority who are naturals and simply cannot be stopped from leading. Whatever context they find themselves in, they end up at the front, and with the passing of years their influence increases beyond comprehension. Second, there are leaders who take initiative and responsibility only for what they have to. These leaders will never be anything more. Third, there are the majority of people who, with the appropriate nurture through training and mentoring, will develop to be quality leaders. That is the group that we are a part of. Gallup research among over ten thousand leaders in the UK has shown that 90 per cent of leaders emerge before they are thirty by taking initiative and responsibility. The Evangelical Alliance's Commission on Strategic Evangelism has identified a generation gap in the church of those aged twenty-one to forty years old. They suggest that resources to reach and train this generation should be a strategic focus for the church in this age. It is therefore so important that you are reading this book.

I believe that God's desire is to raise up a new generation of leaders who are not going to settle for building the kingdom in ghettos, but who are going to break out and build the kingdom in the world. There are going to be politicians, teachers, business people, musicians, lawyers and medics who will have a heart to see their profession, society and friends overcome with the presence of God.

Which is where this book comes in. Destiny is about the seven habits that are going to be found in all the most effective influencers who are leading the way into the twenty-first century. It's about the passion and the purpose, the common sense and the inspiration. If we want to make a difference, if we want to be the ones holding the pen rather than the ones reading the paper, we need to discover our full potential.

But why seven, you ask. To be honest I'm not sure why, but I can tell you how. You see, it's all taken a long time, and over the years I've thought long and hard about destiny and God. In trying to work out what it means to discover it, some conclusions I've come up with have been intuitive insights into leadership, some have come from observations on contemporary culture, while others have been drawn from the personal experience of emerging as a leader and getting to grips with the various struggles and the challenges along the way. At times I've thought about and analysed both outmoded and fresh models of management and leadership, while at others I've just sat down and asked God why we seem to have such a problem living integrated lives in the church, home and in the marketplace. The ideas that have formed out of this smorgasbord of experience – as well as having been interpreted through the lens of the Bible and the kingdom of God as demonstrated by Jesus Christ – point clearly towards the fundamentals of the Christian faith at the same time as pushing against a few of the unnecessary boundaries that we've erected there.

In case it helps, I've thrown in a few stories about how I've been trying to discover my own destiny – it's taking time, but if I look hard enough I think I can see it forming. I suppose at the end of the day I've done this because I'm utterly convinced that we need a generation of Christians who are going to work to build the kingdom of God in the workplace as well as in the church. So please, read on and act upon what hits you between the eyes. Don't drift through life, discover the destiny you were created to live.

1

The Journeyer

So I'm sitting on this tube train on my way to a meeting in London, when a young bloke gets on and sits down opposite me. No prizes for guessing his religion, I think, and go back to my paper. I'm not doing so well on the Times Two Crossword and I can't resist another look, so I take in the classic combination of shorts, socks and sandals. As if they weren't clue enough, his Day-Glo tee shirt screams the message, 'FOLLOW ME OR GO TO HELL' beneath a picture of Jesus with a Kalashnikov and a persuasive look in his eye. I have a sudden desire to finish the crossword.

He had sat down next to a couple of blokes who I assumed he must have known, and had been talking to them for a couple of stops. Looking up again I realise that they don't know him and, judging by the sideways glances and folded arms, they're not that fussed about getting to know him either. He's leaning over them, prodding with his finger and staring at them with an even more maniacal look than the Jesus on his tee shirt. He's telling them about Jesus and God and the very real certainty that they will one day have to give account for all they've done in their lives. Not quite the way that I'd go about evangelism perhaps, but he seems to be keen.

A couple more stops though, and I'm feeling uncomfortable. Having been through what seems like all of the Messianic prophesies, Mr Jesus-with-a-Kalashnikov has now moved on to the subject of supermarkets – or Satanmarkets as he prefers to call them. Most of the carriage are now watching and the two blokes are staring blankly into space in an attempt to put him off by pretending to have slipped into a coma. It's not working.

'You just have to be so so so careful,' he says, spitting out his words at 100 m.p.h. 'The Prince of Darkness is in those places and he has got them in his grip through the use of bar codes which – did you know? – are based on three sets of numbers, each one adding up to six, so when you get to the end you have six-six-six which is the mark of the beast, and if you shop there you will be caught up in his web of deceit for he is the …'

I imagine that when he finally does let them go and they make their way home, they will be left with a terrible impression of Christianity. They'll probably be ripping it out of Christians for weeks. I can't say I blame them, but maybe I can do something about it.

'That is a load of rubbish,' I say, interrupting him midway through a speech on the spiritual dangers of listening to early Wham! tracks. Silence.

He turns his eyes towards me and, leaving his first victims, moves in for the kill. He takes the book of Revelation as his main weapon and starts quoting random chunks in an effort to prove his Satanmarket theory. I'm suddenly extremely glad of my years spent at Bible college and point out that he has misinterpreted the original Greek.

'Greek?' he snorts. 'But it's written in English.' I can tell he thinks he's met an idiot. At last we agree on something. He tells me that I need to be born again, to accept Jesus into my life and confess my sins. I tell him I have already, that I love Jesus and pray to be filled with the Holy Spirit every day. His jaw drops, and for the first time since Wimbledon he looks unsure of himself. Most of the carriage are watching and listening intently, wondering whether we're about to start battling like two crazed monsters in a Japanese animation.

'But you can't possibly be a Christian,' he informs me. When I ask why, he tells me that Christians are supposed to love each other and that I clearly don't love him.

'I do love you,' I reply. 'But I'm just really embarrassed that you call yourself a Christian.' The carriage full of people seem to find this rather amusing and it certainly seems to put an end to his advances. He gets off at the next stop with a passing comment about me going to hell. I just about resist pointing out that I am actually on my way to South Kensington.

A little further on and it's time for the original two blokes to get off. As they leave they shake my hand and say thank you, and I'm left with the hope that tonight, instead of talking about how sad Christians are, they might talk about something else instead.

Don't worry, this isn't going to be one of those books full of victorious stories of me cleaning up the streets like some kind of spiritual equivalent of De Niro in *Taxi Driver*. There are plenty of times when I've been more like tee shirt man, running around on a cocktail of confusion and spiritual earnestness. I've made mistakes and been a fool, partly (I think) because of the way that I have relied on an outdated modus operandi.

Today, life is far more about journey, adventure and discovery than it is about dogma, doctrine and absolutes; it is less important to try and persuade someone that they are wrong – like train man did – than it is to embrace the spirit of the quest and enjoy the sense of discovery. Of course, this shift in boundaries brings with it a pick-'n'-mix selection of good and not so good stuff; of things that we Christians can go along with, and things that we find difficult. The point of being a journeyer on the way to destiny today is being ready to accept the challenges that face us daily, not with fixed ideas but with an open mind and a desire for God to reveal the truth.

The Season of Truth

A little more about that change: at one time reason was god. Science and rational thought were the big boys in the neighbourhood and there was nothing anyone could do to get rid of them. This period always makes me think of university, for it is there that people spend time researching their thesis, looking for and finding the answers, regurgitating them in their finals and walking off with a certificate that says 'well done' at the end. University is all about discovering facts and your own truths: whether they be philosophical, academic or alcoholic.

Today we've moved on from the modern culture as personified by universities and have plonked ourselves down at a place that is suitably called the postmodern era. This philosophical and moral car boot sale can be likened to the New Age movement. Instead of dealing in absolutes, it focuses on a range of spiritual experiences, points to the otherness of life and praises existential experience. Arriving at the phrase 'I feel therefore I am', we see that post-modernism is much less about truth and more about discovery. My friend Laurence articulates the postmodern world-view so clearly when he summarises it as the perspective that everything is right, and nothing is wrong, apart from saying you are right.

But what is a good Christian to do? Should we hold back the joss-sticked winds of change and stand firm on the truth? In a sense the answer is yes; there are some truths that we can never deny. But do we really know all there is to know about God? What about ourselves – is there more to discover? Getting to know God and ourselves is a journey, one which is marked out by the purpose that God has for us, by the discoveries he is waiting for us to make. Because of this there is room for us to embrace the spirit of discovery and the adventure of life.

When I turned thirty years old I realised that my journey was whizzing by and I decided that I needed to refocus my priorities. One of the things I did was to write a personal mission statement. Eventually I came up with: 'To live the great adventure of life in all its fullness with God'. As I looked over the last thirty years of my life it was clear that it had been an adventure and I'm sure now that from what I know of God it is only just beginning.

I didn't think I was that smart at school so I left when I was sixteen. I got a job with the Ministry of Defence in Farnborough, Hampshire. I was working in electronics and computing and I really enjoyed it. There seemed to be a pretty clear path opening up ahead of me and in time I became an officer and worked in the Admiralty on the Trident submarines. Somewhere in the middle of it all I became a Christian and was captivated by God. It was as if he had taken hold of me and I had taken hold of him. We started a journey together, and it didn't take long for me to suss out that my values and ambitions had undergone a pretty significant change. I had a nice office, plenty of travel, loads of career prospects and a pay cheque that was swelling nicely. Yet something changed and I no longer felt comfortable with things. It was an intensely competitive working environment, and if I did stay I would have to succeed. The idea of being forty, having a big house and steady job in the MoD suddenly seemed uninspiring. Better holidays, bigger wardrobes and faster cars came into perspective and I wanted to do something more.

To my mind – young and inexperienced as it was – I felt the best way for me to go out and do something worthwhile was to work for the church. I dutifully attended Bible college for a year and looked around for someone to employ me. Eventually I ended up as minister of three churches in Yorkshire, discovering with time that the job was a mixture of the good and the bad.

Looking back now it's clear how naive I was to believe that serving God meant wearing a dog-collar. I was wrong: it's neither the only way nor the best way. These days I'm fond of saying that we live life forward, but only understand it looking back. It's something unique about experience – especially that which doesn't taste so sweet – that makes it so able to shape and direct. It's only from a distance that we can see what it has formed.

Thinking about life in terms of a journey, I'm sure that working for the church wasn't the only path that I could have taken. I believe now that we can serve God wherever we are, regardless of the fringe benefits or accompanying difficulties. For a God who is so obviously intent on building not just the church but the kingdom in the world, it must have been slightly frustrating to have me suggest to him that the best way to serve was to enter 'the ministry' of the church. There is nowhere in the world where God cannot be actively at work and no place where he doesn't want his kingdom to break out in all its glorious reality.

If we want our corporate destiny to be seeing this kingdom built then we need a whole generation of people who are able to tune into God at the same time as stacking shelves. So, you may ask, does that mean that we need to learn how to hum choruses at the same time as serving fries? Should we be longing for the next tea break so that we can dose up on a bit of ministry in the stationery cupboard? Thankfully not. Being ready to get real with God in the workplace means being able to see the value that he places on our work and interaction with the world. It means learning a type of Christianity that is truly relevant to every sphere of the world of work. We need to be smart and able to put Christian values and beliefs to work at the very heart of our society. From politics to the arts, medicine to the service industry, if we're not speaking and acting for God through those industries, then how will his voice be heard and his heart be made known?

The Great Divide

I've known Fiona for about ten years and over the course of time we've seen each other grow and change, take on new challenges and work our way through hard choices. There have been plenty of times since I've known her when Fiona has had the opportunity to land herself a job within the church, either as a youth leader, pastoral worker or minister. Instead, she has stuck with her training (when we first met she was studying to be a nurse) and has gone into the health service, inspired by a belief that God actively wants her to be right at the heart of the system, working hard to bring about change, affecting values and policies that mould the way the whole thing works.

Looking at it now it's obvious that she's in the right place, but at every stage, church work exerted a gravitational pull the size of Venus. Not that there is anything wrong with it but, for Fiona, working for the church was the easy option: she knew that success – as measured by a decidedly human set of standards – was guaranteed. She would be in a public position, receiving attention for doing things that were obviously 'of the Lord'. Working in the health service, however, was a different matter altogether, with moral and ethical quandaries testing her faith to the limit and absolutely no chance to rack up a decent tally of on-the-job conversions.

Fiona's dilemma is sadly not unusual. I met someone at a conference recently who, having told me that she was on the verge of completing a degree in media and journalism, was wondering whether to pursue it and find work on a magazine or 'do something for God'. It's absurd that we have downloaded this assumption that work that pleases God only ever fits into a dog-collar, especially when the obvious need for us to be involved in every sphere of society is so pressing and is so clearly on God's heart.

We do this because we find it strangely easy to compartmentalise our lives. With all the skill of a warehouse picker and packer, we separate the whole of our lives into subsections, avoiding any risk of cross-contamination. We create separate areas for work, home, friends, family, education and church, declaring that God is in some but that others are unholy tasks that have to be carried out under sufferance. Is it any wonder that Christianity and the church seem so irrelevant to people? This generation needs to bust out of fragmented life and find for ourselves an integrated life, one where we see God as being involved in every area of our daily routine and outlook on life.

This sorry state has roots that go back to ancient Greek philosophy. Thinkers such as Plato considered the material realm evil and to be escaped from. By contrast, anything that could be deemed spiritual was automatically considered good and godly. The church – thus influenced by Greek thought – has unwittingly done a good job of preserving these beliefs down the centuries, and they have eaten away at Christianity, stunting growth and damaging progress.

This concept was enforced by the so-called Great Reformation – a time when the protesting church separated from the state. The separation of sacred and secular gave the Protestant church an excuse to relinquish its grip on politics and the life of the people. Even in this century we have seen the Evangelical church focusing on spiritual life and the Charismatic church on the spiritual gifts, making 'the world' out to be the enemy. We need to rediscover the Jewish roots of Christianity – with prayers to be said at work and prayers to be said while on the toilet – where God is involved in every area of life.

Sadly this message of separation has filtered through to popular culture, and London's Millennium Dome features individual areas for fun, science, transaction and so on. It is only in the Spirit Zone that we find God and the representation of faith. Surely God wants to be a part of every zone of our lives? What's more, I'm convinced that the rise in religions such as Islam points to the fact that there are plenty of other people out there who feel the same. Islam has avoided the compartmentalisation of God and perhaps that is one of the reasons why it is experiencing growth in Western society.

For the journeyer this is the future. The task lies ahead of us; the route uncertain but the destination assured, the first steps so critical in moving forward. An ancient Chinese proverb says that 'a journey of a thousand miles begins with a single step'. As founder of the computer giant Microsoft, Bill Gates understands the importance of making the first steps. Already the richest man in the world, Gates is steadily moving towards his vision of putting a Microsoft-operated computer in every home, believing that 'success is a journey, not a destination'.

I'm involved in a prayer triplet. Surprisingly, there are three of us and we get together to pray. Paul is a business consultant and Giles is a manager in a hospital. Recently Giles was facing a difficult time in his career. He was up for a reorganisation of departments and it looked as though he was going to take responsibility for a Termination of Pregnancy (TOPs) unit. As a Christian, Giles is understandably pro-life, and the prospect of managing a unit that performed so many abortions, albeit doing it as professionally and efficiently as he could, was something that had him worried. Could he take the position with integrity? How did his faith respond to such an extreme test? It turned out that someone else took the position in the unit, but the issue is bound to re-surface. As he progresses along the career path, Giles knows that he will have to face similar issues again.

Like any good journey, we don't know every contour and view when we start out. These things will come in time and so, for Giles, not having the answers now is not necessarily a bad thing. There will be issues that will confuse and frustrate each of us along the way, but we cannot be expected to have all the answers to hand right from the start.

The working life that many of us lead is not black and white like it can be in the church where the right decision is clearly distinguishable from the wrong one.

In reality it's mostly grey; confused and hard to decipher. The workplace is signposted with complex moral decisions and dilemmas. It is a real struggle to know which is the right decision to make. It is so often not a choice between right and wrong but a choice between the tough and the tougher.

Daniel is a fantastic example of someone who didn't live in a black and white environment where decisions were easy and the truth was clear. He lived in the grey, having been taken from his own culture and placed in a foreign city where he was made to learn a new language, live in an alien environment and eat strange food. Having moved to Babylon, his name (as well as the names of his friends) was changed to one which sounded like a foreign god, and he was made to study Babylonian culture, including the worship of many gods. He took it all, but for some reason when it came to his diet he refused to go along with the plan. Sticking to a strictly vegetarian diet, he rejected the rich food of the king's table and ended up in better shape than all the other students. Like Daniel, we too need to know how to continue living in the grey, where little is clear, but at the same time knowing exactly when is the right time to draw the line and declare our boundaries.

There were three men working on a building site. A passing stranger got curious and asked each in turn what they were doing.

'I'm just laying the bricks until I can go home and relax,' says the first.

'I'm here to earn some cash to look after my family,' says the second.

'Me?' says the third. 'I'm building a cathedral.'

This is how it can be. The nine to five routine is for some of us a way of passing time or putting food on the table. For others it can be about the best of life. I am convinced that God wants us to understand that whatever we are doing we are building his kingdom, spreading about some of his good-Godness in the world. Here we come across the difference between having a job and having a vocation. Knowing that you are called to something, knowing that God is using you in what you are doing is one of the most important steps that the journeyer takes. This fundamental shift in attitude produces an equally fundamental change in the way we view work. It was a lesson that took me a long while to learn, but now, as a director of a charity, Joshua Generation, I feel that I've begun to understand it. What's more, I hope that in the not-too-distant future that I'll be operating in the marketplace as well as operating in the church scene. I believe the most effective twenty-first century Christian will be on a journey with God through life and will be able to journey between the church and marketplace with ease. The species of jobs for life is extinct; people in the marketplace retrain several times during their careers for different jobs. Why should the church be any different?

I love the story of Abraham, called at a (less than) ripe old age to be a blessing to many nations and an all-round great man. There was no accompanying A to Z, no detailed list of hostels and hotels, no assurance of breaks, rests and periods of recreation. Some would say that he had earned his right to a quiet life, and that perhaps God should have turned up a few decades earlier to start his journey. But God had a plan for him as he does for us.

Joseph was a great journeyer. Half the time he didn't have a clue what was happening to him. He seemed to be the victim of others' decisions: his brothers' jealousy-fuelled idea to sell him into slavery, the spurned lust of Potiphar's wife. When things went well it was largely due to divine intervention; especially when God gave him the interpretation of the Pharaoh's dream. That led him to assume the role of prime minister of the country of Egypt, and he may well have thought by then his journey had reached its destination. He could be forgiven for that and I'm sure many of us would think the same, but in fact, God's plan went even further. His divine purpose was that through Joseph's obedience, his people would be saved from famine. It was only at the very end of his life that he learnt what it had all been about.

The story follows on a while later and takes in the life and times of Moses. I think the film *Prince of Egypt* captured it pretty well, exploring the confusion that he must have gone through. Born a Hebrew but brought up an Egyptian, he married a Midianite and quite understandably asked God, 'Who am I?' Moses was confused about his identity and his journey was certainly making no sense whatsoever but despite that he was every inch a man of destiny. Moses was born for a purpose, and without any one of the jigsaw pieces that made up his person perhaps the story would have been different.

The Uncertainty of Life

I was recently travelling to Germany in what I thought would be the safety of British Airways. There were only about twenty-five of us waiting in the departure lounge, and I was looking forward to getting a bank of seats all to myself. I wasn't in luck for the plane was straight out of WWI – a twin-prop plane with seats only slightly better than benches. This could be fun, I thought, as I found a seat down the front.

We taxied onto the runway, but seemed to pause before starting our take-off. I was about to start playing with the life-jacket when the stewardess came and asked myself and the other man sitting at the front if we wouldn't mind moving to the back to help redistribute weight for take-off. This had me nearly as scared as the other passengers who wondered what was wrong with the front seats. I spent the rest of the flight practising the crash position and trying to get the oxygen mask down.

For the rest of us, our own journeys are marked by similar moments when we too question whether we are going to make it to our destination. It can all seem so hard, so fraught with danger that the possibility of arrival seems to be about as likely as the possibility of me ever flying with BA again. What's more, to be sure of reaching our destination goes against the cultural grain; where the quest is God, where the state of questioning is everything, then arrival is an almost irrelevant concept. Where we stand apart as Christians is that we have a very real certainty of our destination. We know where God is taking us in the long term (into a new heaven and earth), but we also know the direction that we must be travelling in the short term (towards Jesus). We may not be sure of how we are going to get there, but emulating Jesus – his life of self-sacrifice and communion with God – is the way to go about it. In this way we share something with Mulder and Scully of the X-Files: the truth is out there somewhere. They are looking for it, trying to sift through the mass of conspiracies and supernaturals, and we too search for it through the haze of faith, history and transcendental experience.

Of course, while being on a journey with God, with all the accompanying uncertainties and difficulties, it is vital that we trust and know that he is in charge. We need to consider that he has a unique purpose for us, that we have a valuable part to play. If we see ourselves as disposable, if we believe that our pursuit of the goal is neither here nor there, that our contribution to God's big picture is worth little, then we will give up at the first sign of trouble. That would be a tragedy.

We are sometimes known as Generation X – the generation who lack purpose and meaning at the core of their lives. Tempting as it might be to think it, we are not alone. We share a direct link with God's people in the Old Testament. They too felt alone and utterly lacking in direction, and when they were taken from their home city and exported en masse, the prophet Jeremiah arose and delivered some righteous truth. ' "I know the plans I have for you," declares the Lord, "plans to prosper you and not to harm you, plans to give you hope and a future" ' (Jeremiah 29:11). Even for those weary people who wondered where on earth God was in their disaster, out of God's heart came a message of hope, purpose and meaning. We need to get us some of that too, and quick.

Often as Christians we subscribe to the theory that to be holy means to have nothing to do with that dirty world on the other side of the vestry. In fact, we sometimes consider that our best option is to speak out against it all the time, pointing out the faults, flaws and signs of a fallen world. Unfortunately, rather than hating it, God actually loves the world – a fact which he proved by sending his Son down to a horrendous death. Being God's children means that we get to share in that fatherly love, meaning that we too have something of Jesus's purpose to our lives. We are here to save the world back for him, to exhibit that same sacrificial attitude, that same compassion, that same love. Sounds tough, yes? It is, because we will not influence the world from the safety of our church meetings but rather through our working lives in the marketplace.

As a journeying generation ready to get stuck into the world we need to understand how Jesus would have done it. Now this is a tricky one, as the Bible doesn't say an awful lot about how Jesus conducted himself when he was a chippie. What we do know, though, is that when he was more into the sales market he was totally honest, caring and loving. He took time out to be with the underdog and did whatever he promised. In your workplace is there room to follow his lead? How will you honour your contracts? How will you treat the office geek? Will you work for the cash or play for the team? Will you avoid the tricky decisions, or will you be like Jesus and put yourself in among the toughest issues? He made sure that he was right at the heart of things by debating with the Pharisees and religious leaders.

One of the most exciting times that I can remember hearing people talk about vocation and their future was on a flight to Malta. I was sat behind a group of people who had just finished their GCSEs and were heading out for a little R and R. The question they were asking themselves was the question that we have all asked ourselves at some point: What are you going to be when you grow up? Between them they came up with just about every aspiration you could imagine: from the next Richard Branson to a builder, from the next Spice Girl to a lawyer. They were all pretty intense about it, excited by the things they felt they knew were just around the corner.

It got me thinking too, asking myself what my life for God is going to be about. How can we work it out? How can we even know where we should start the journey? It dawned on me that the only way to find out our God-given destiny is to give him all we can. That doesn't mean handing over just 10 per cent of what we earn or trudging along to cell group because there's nothing better to do. Giving your life to God means grabbing hold of him and saying an almighty 'yes'. It is about telling God that you are up for anything, whatever the cost, whatever the time.

Perhaps that seems a little too much. Maybe it all looks good on paper but the transfer from text to life just leaves you cold. Not that we're in it for the glory, but it's worth considering that history remembers the passionate ones. Take William Wallace, subject of the film *Braveheart*. He spent his life on freeing his fellow countrymen from the tyranny of the English. Even when facing death – the choice of a public denial of all he stood for in return for a quick death or painful torture – he chose to hold on to what he had lived for. As the film closes we see him hung until he can barely breathe and drawn out on a rack so that all his joints are dislocated. Finally, as his stomach is cut open, his intestines removed, and his body cut in quarters he cries out with his last breath the word that sends shivers down my spine: 'Freedom'. That was what his life was about.

When I turned thirty I had a bit of an early mid-life crisis. I made a number of lifestyle decisions, one of which was my diet and exercise routine, which had to happen before my waist completely took over and the Pierre Cardin DJ would never fit again. The low-fat diet of salad and chicken, pasta and tuna lacks the thrill of Indian cuisine and cheeses with my wine. The snowboarding game for my playstation went back in the box and the bike was enticed out of retirement. Then the 15-mile rides around Wimbledon Common and Richmond Park nearly killed me. It's interesting that Paul describes this Christian journey that we are on as a race, for with my new-look motivational approach to life, I began to see what he was getting at. It was hard work and demanded discipline but I lost kilos and centimetres. Both spiritual and physical health require determination, perseverance and discipline to keep going until we reach the goal. *The Message*, a contemporary translation of the Bible, puts it like this:

You've all been to the stadium and seen the athletes race. Everyone runs; one wins. Run to win. All good athletes train hard; they do it for a gold medal that tarnishes and fades. You're after one that's gold eternally. I don't know about you but I'm running hard for the finish line, I'm giving it everything I've got. No sloppy living for me – I'm staying alert and in top condition. I'm not going to get caught napping, telling everyone else all about it and then missing out myself. (See 1 Corinthians 9:25-7)

Not that I have already obtained all this, or have already been made perfect, but I press on to take hold of that for which Christ Jesus took hold of me. Brothers, I do not consider myself yet to have taken hold of it. But one thing I do: Forgetting what is behind and straining towards what is ahead, I press on towards the goal to win the prize for which God has called me heavenwards in Christ Jesus. (Philippians 3:12–14)

This journey that we're all on demands our hard graft. We have to work at it to move forwards, finding the perseverance that will keep us going. That persistence is something that pleases God, for he knows how important it is to the journey. Jonathan Edwards (the alive triple jumper rather than the dead revivalist) talks about the feeling that when he competes well he pleases God. It's the same for all of us; God loves to see us move forward, no matter what stage we are at in the race.

This journey is a race, one with competitors and hurdles. We must keep going without flinching or giving up, even when the going gets really tough. Whenever I read about this in the Bible I always remember the film *Forest Gump* where Tom Hanks' character is picked on while walking home from school. Hoping that he can avoid the stones being hurled at him, his friend Jenny shouts, 'Run, Forest, run!' That is what I imagine God saying: 'Run, Matt, run!'

We need to focus ourselves on running the race and completing it. Recently I attended a management and leadership seminar which drew on sports psychology as one of the sources for its teaching. They mentioned some research which had asked top athletes how important they believed psychological factors were in the outcome of a competition once they were in physical condition. The athletes responded that 70 to 90 per cent of the outcome is based on psychological factors. We need to visualise the race that is before us and imagine completing it, and then do it.

If we are to discover our destiny by the great journey that God has in store for us we need to surrender everything that we are and everything that we ever hope to be to God. Jesus said that if anyone wants to follow him they must lay down their own life and take up their cross daily. Those who lose their lives to him will discover what life is truly about. If we want to know what our destiny is then we need to do the same as we chase and pursue him.

Action

1 What work are you doing at the moment? Do you see it as a job or a vocation? How could you change the way you view your work so that it becomes a vocation that you can serve God through?

2 What are some of the obstacles and hurdles that you have faced in the last year of journeying with God? Pray, and thank God that he has brought you through these. Next time you feel cornered, remember God has got you through before.

3 Design your own mission statement by writing down things that you think are important to your own journey of life. Stick this somewhere you will see it

every day, perhaps in the front of your Bible or behind the toilet door.

4 What can you do in your life to show God, and the people who know you, that you are getting serious and sacrificial with Jesus in a new way? This might be something practical or something symbolic – like giving away your annual bonus. Just do it.

2

The Lover

I've just been reminded of something. It was the middle of 1995 and I had known her for five days. We were on a trip around the lakes of northern Italy, getting lost on the way to well-signposted monasteries and worrying that the water might not be safe to drink. I'd had my eye on her since Luton, and I was pretty sure that I had been reading the signs correctly.

It was a Christian holiday and I was supposed to be leading. That meant I was the one who: copped the flack when the bags went missing (which they did at Pisa); refused to pay the bill when a drunken waiter expressed an interest in getting to know the wife of the Vicar of St Arnold's in Dibden-Under-Wolde (which happened frequently); and who conveyed the group's sense of disappointment to the monks that they were yet to catch up with the Toronto Blessing (despite the attempt of several members of the group to lay hands on the monsignor during mass).

But there was a plus side to all this. I got to travel to another country, drank some fine wine and ended up as a confidant and shoulder to cry on for many of the holidaymakers. Which is where she comes in. As I said, she first caught my attention at the airport. While the others were busy fretting over their baggage allowances, she was quietly sat on her case reading through some psalms. Throughout the trip she'd been pretty much the same – quiet and relaxed, choosing to spend time on the edge of the group as opposed to joining in the rounds of waiter-baiting or monkicide. She was old enough to be my grandmother, and we had some good chats over the week, so much so that I'd go so far as to say that I trusted her judgment and was keen to ask her advice on a few things. Just as I had worked this out, she came over to where I was sitting. Slightly startled, I stood up.

'Matt,' she said. 'I think I have a word for you.'

I knew it, I thought to myself. I knew she was prophetic. I de-tensed my shoulders and waited for it to come. I was guessing that it would be about the journey I was on with God – but what exactly, I was unsure. Would she prophesy about my work or would she tell me who I'm going to marry?

'The Lord says that he'd like you a lot more if you got rid of your earring.'

I laughed. She didn't. I squinted my eyes and turned

my head on one side, offering a half smile that said, 'Go on – tell me you're joking.'

She slowly closed her eyes and told me to weigh it up and allow my heart to receive the truth. 'Correction,' she added, 'can be hard to accept, Matt. But sin is sin and it must be burnt out like a wart.'

She was long gone by the time I'd recovered enough to ask her if she'd read Deuteronomy lately. If she hadn't legged it I would have reminded her of the bit where it mentions the slaves who – in the seventh year when they were given the option of freedom – chose to remain with their masters and had their ear pierced as a sign of their commitment to them. Somewhere along the line this lady completely missed the point of what Christianity is all about. It's the relationship not the rules of religion that is important. The rest of the holiday passed without incident and the continued presence of my earring seemed to make her even more remote.

It's frighteningly easy for us Christians to catch religion rather than fall for God. When the religious fat cats of Jesus's time questioned him about what he thought was the most important principle to live by, he replied, ' "Love the Lord your God with all your heart and with all your soul and with all your mind." This is the first and greatest commandment. And the second is like it: "Love your neighbour as you love yourself" ' (Matthew 22:37–9).

It takes an active decision to love God in the first place. The bit at the very heart of Christianity is an intense and passionate burning love that draws us further in towards God.

This memory has waddled its way back to the front of my mind because of a young man named Simon. He's spending a few days travelling around with me to see if he'd like to get into doing a bit of preaching himself. So far, it has been interesting. You see, Simon's keen on getting things right. That's no bad thing in itself, but it has brought up a fair amount of uptight intensity since his arrival.

I feel like I'm on *Mastermind* and my specialist subject is theological rhetoric. We've had it all; from my position on eschatology to the ordination of women. Just now we've been through a quick-fire round of that old classic, 'Call Yourself a Christian?'. Questions asked have been: Do I really believe that I can give glory to God when I'm dressed in garments other than the ubiquitous navy blue suit from Next? How can I call myself a Christian when I don't evangelise on trains? I've had the patience to respond to most of the questions but I guess I'm not anally retentive enough to take it all so seriously. Simon is one of those fundamentalists who thinks there is a Bible text directly relevant for every situation. I resist asking him what he thinks of all that biblical genocide, rape and bigamy, for fear of another heavy and intense discussion. I like meeting people who know what they believe – but I also like people who are human. It seems to me that Simon is missing the point. He is so wrapped up with the book and the rules that he misses the relationship and the love.

Eventually I just have to say something to him. 'Simon, are you planning on getting married?'

'Well, taking a pre-lapsarian view of the . . .'

'It's a yes-or-no kind of question, Simon.'

'Yes.'

'Good. When you do get married, will you love your wife or your wedding vows?'

He takes a deep breath as if to release another hurricane diatribe. He pauses. 'My wife.'

That's my point. A person can't love paper and ink; they can only love a person. A husband loves his wife, not his wedding vows. In the same way Christians love God, not the Bible. The Bible is inspired and we live by the example of God's relationship with his people that it gives us, but we can't have a relationship with a book.

Master of the Outrageous

A lot of people like to attach a fair amount of peripheral stuff to the heart of Christianity. For me it's the stark difference between religion and relationship with God. Jesus met people like this too, and knew exactly how they felt about things. It was a real shame that the Pharisees didn't catch on that Jesus was refocusing their faith – they were among the most devout, the most committed people around, and if they hadn't let their rules get in the way, they could have gone so far with Jesus. Things ended up with them plotting to kill him and Jesus telling them that while they confessed God with their lips, they missed the point because their hearts were a long way off. Sadly, their determination to follow religion left them inflexible, and they totally missed out on the most amazing opportunity of forgiveness and a relationship with the Son of God. As Jesus said, they had let go of the commands of God and were holding on to the traditions of men. What's more, the tradition of watching the sea but missing the wave failed to die out with the Pharisees, and is alive and well today. There's a danger in all of this that we focus solely on the mistakes and broken rules that people make and ignore the goodness on offer – the outrageous love of God.

I love going up to the West End and visiting the theatres. A big favourite has to be *Les Misérables*. If you don't know the plot, it's basically the story of one man's fight to redeem himself. The story starts as Jean Val Jean is released on parole after nineteen years on the chain gang. However, the freedom is only partial as he is bound by law to present his parole certificate wherever he goes, resulting in virtually everyone treating him like an outcast. I say virtually everyone, as the Bishop of Digne takes him in and lays on a spread of his best food and wine, offering him a bed for the night. In the early hours Jean repays the bishop by helping himself to the best silver and heads out of town. As luck would have it he gets caught and, not looking too much like the sort of man who would legally be carrying a sack full of clerical silver around in the dead of night, they take him back to the bishop to sort things out. To everyone's surprise the bishop welcomes him like a friend and explains to the cops that the silver was a gift. What's more, he goes on to tell Jean off for forgetting to take the silver candlesticks as well. He gives him the lot and sends him on his way. After that, Jean goes free and rebuilds his life. From that point on – the moment of outrageous love that was totally undeserved – he decides to live differently.

So, no prizes for guessing what that bit reminds me of. (In case you're wondering, it's God.) You see, relationship is everything – without it Christianity is little more than (as Eddie Izzard says) 'mumbling in cold buildings'. Jean Val Jean certainly didn't deserve the love shown to him by the bishop, and you and I don't deserve the immense love of God either, but to ignore his offer of relationship – to turn around and say, 'Oh yeah, thanks for your Son's life and death and all that, but I'll just stick to being a good person, if you don't mind' – is pure stupidity.

I don't claim to know all the words to Auld Lang Syne, and I haven't got a clue what the song's going on about, but I'm well into New Year's Eve. Me and Hogmanay get on famously, especially when it's fuelled by loads of friends and a bottle of wine or two. When I was a minister this presented itself as a bit of a problem. After having a great time celebrating things old and new at a midnight service at church, I used to sprint across the road to the pub before they shut the doors for the lock-in. The locals were chuffed to have the vicar in on their celebrations and prized themselves on buying me drinks. Most of the church saw no problem in this – after all, I wasn't going there to get off my face – but there were a few that thought my choice of location for the celebrations slightly unsuitable. Now I've spent hours mulling this one over, and I can't for the life of me work out why it was such a faux pas. I can only conclude that it has something to do with not following the rules; but where does the Bible say pubs and parties are wrong, anyway?

If you want a slightly more dramatic example of this kind of thing, consider Tony Campolo. The American professor and speaker had the astounding privilege of taking on the role of personal minister to President Clinton. Through the dark days of the Kenneth Starr investigation, our Tony got to visit Bill for an hour or so every other week. Can you imagine that? What a privilege, what an opportunity. Even if you forget the fact that it was with the leader of the most powerful nation in the world, isn't spending time talking things through with someone whose life is spiralling out of control exactly one of the things we Christians should be doing?

Instead of unanimous support, Tony Campolo received – again from a vocal minority – criticism and condemnation. It's amazing that Christians could slam him for spending time with a sinner and not realise the outrageous foolishness of their words.

Jesus loved the unlovable. He spent time with them, making detours and alterations to his itinerary so that he could be with them. They made him late and gave him a bad reputation. They also were the classroom where he taught his most revolutionary lessons: love the poor, put others before yourself, respect the lowly.

King David was a special kind of guy. Like a terrier catching a sniff of a squirrel, David was after God's heart. He wanted to know him, follow him and love him. Not surprisingly God loved him for it. But as well as being one of the most important kings in Israel's history, he was also responsible for one of the juiciest screw-ups. His failure started when he decided not to go to war with the other men. This does not mean that I class all peace-loving vegetarians as failures, but it does mean that I think that, for David, having too much time on his hands and being on his own was a bad thing. He ended up mooching around the palace, and when temptation came his way he was not in a strong position to resist.

Of course, temptation wasn't far away, and when he spied Bathsheba taking a bath he acted on impulse and invited her up to his quarters for a bit of slap and tickle. Following their affair he found out that she was pregnant, so David ordered Bathsheba's husband Uriah to be sent to the front line where he met his certain death. His failure was therefore complete – and comprehensive, much like ours. Sin will always take us further than we want to go and cost us more than we are willing to pay. But God still loved David, and allowed him to know that love which he expressed alongside his deep remorse and repentance in Psalm 51.

There are plenty of people around today who have made horrendous mistakes, and none of us like the idea of everyone finding out about those dark, hidden things that we've tried so hard to forget. None of us are that different, and yet none of us are too far away from God's outrageous love.

I was working in the East End of London when I met a community worker. She had the look of someone who had come up against too many brick walls, someone who knew disappointment only too well. The stories she told about her job confirmed this: working with people caught for years in the poverty trap, unable to get work that would support them as the benefits were cut away. At times it seemed as though the whole system was against her and her clients. Still, on the day that I met her, she told me that she was pretty happy. One of her clients – a single mother kept prisoner in a decaying high-rise block – had recently received a telephone bill that threatened to cripple her. There was no way she could pay the amount, and although she admitted that she was responsible and was prepared to face the consequences, the implications for her and her innocent daughter were enormous. In desperation, the community worker called the phone company on her client's behalf. She told them about her financial status, and hoped that they might be able to come up with some sort of compromise.

'Well,' said the operator at the end of the line, 'there is another way we can help. Write the following reference number on the bill and the words "FEE WAIVED" on the top and send it to me. We'll write this one off for you.'

Of course everyone was amazed and ecstatic, and the company's generosity had a dramatic effect on the young mother. As I heard the story, it resonated with me about the way that God has forgiven our debts and through his Son Jesus Christ has declared to us . . . fee waived.

This sort of forgiveness is a profound demonstration of the outrageous love that God has for us, and that we need so desperately. It reminds me of the Beatles song, 'All you need is love'. We tend to think of it as belonging particularly to the blissed-out free-love people of the late 1960s, but the statement is actually a lot more profound than first meets the eye. It's true; love is all you need.

We need love because we have been made in God's image. For those of you unsure of the facts, God the Father, God the Son, and God the Holy Spirit all existed before the Earth did. Theirs was a dynamic relationship, you could even say a community. When they decided to create something that would be like them, the relationship and community bit of things was firmly in the mix. And so here we are – born for relationship with God, and also with each other, just like the blueprint from which we were taken.

In his book *Life after God*, Douglas Coupland retells a story about a young princess who lived in a tower in a castle and fell in love with a travelling prince from a faraway land. Her father was furious, and the king enlisted the help of a witch to brew up a forgetting potion so that his daughter would put the foreigner behind her. The king forced her to drink the potion as his guards held her arms behind her back. As soon as she had swallowed it all, they let go, but she immediately ran to the window and jumped from the tower to her death before the potion could take effect.

Love is so important to us that the prospect of life without it can often seem too much to bear. It is inevitable for us to get hurt as we go through life. When it happens many of us find it hard to love again, scared of allowing ourselves to be vulnerable to another person. The narrator in *Life after God* goes on to describe how, as a younger man, his worries focused on loneliness and the prospect of being unloved. Over time the fears developed into musing about whether or not he would be capable of having an intimate relationship. 'I've felt as though the world lived inside a warm house at night and I was outside and I couldn't be seen because I was out there in the night.'

As the story progresses we see a catalogue of fears mounting up: that love would be dangled in front of him, only to be snatched away as a reaction to his own failings. Solitude offers no solution, as 'unless I explored intimacy and shared intimacy with someone else then life would never progress beyond a certain point. I remember thinking that unless I knew what was going on inside of someone else's head other than my own I was going to explode.' The fear is natural.

When I lived in Sheffield I used to sit at my desk each day and study. I'd made sure that life wasn't all work and had positioned my desk in the middle of the window, giving me a decent view of all that was going on in the street. I should have guessed that this also meant that people had an equally decent view of me but, eventually, that became a good thing.

One day I saw one of my neighbours go past. We hadn't ever spoken, but I recognised her all the same. As she got to the gate, she walked up the path and knocked on the front door. I opened the door and got ready to say hello but saw that she was crying. She told me that all she wanted to do was to stand inside for a few moments. Of course she could, I told her. As she calmed down slightly she explained that she had seen three men ahead of her carrying furniture in the street. She was filled with fear as she remembered how as a child she had been abused by three men in the street. She'd seen me working at my desk day after day, and she thought that she would be safe if she came and knocked on my door.

After a while she left, and later I decided to put a card through her door saying that she should drop in for coffee if ever she wanted, and that she should in no way feel embarrassed about the events of that morning. A few days later she came round and explained how when she came up to the door when she was feeling upset, she was aware of a tremendous sense of love. I told her that the only answer I could find for that was that it had to be the love of God. After all, I'm not naturally soft and compassionate, certainly not to the extent of ever having someone be drawn in like that. It had to be God, and I'm just glad I got to see him working at first hand.

Life is hard, and along the way we will all pick up scars and wounds that may stay with us for years to come. Love is the answer, and whether we know it or not, it is the cure we are all instinctively drawn to.

Mother Theresa, when she was alive, was often the subject of inquisitive journalists' gentle probing. It was rare for any one of them to come straight out and dismiss her as a fool but, reading reports, it's easy to get the picture that they tended to patronise her. After all, this small, frail old nun knew very little about the real world, they thought. She too treated them in accordance with her assumptions about them. There are plenty of priceless quotes going around of conversations where mocking questions like, 'How can you make a difference? It's just a drop in the ocean' are met with knowing smiles and, 'Ah, yes, but an ocean is made up of many drops.'

There's another story that shows the insight of Mother Theresa. She was asked by a Western journalist about the greatest problem in society. She replied, 'The biggest disease today is not leprosy or tuberculosis, but rather the feeling of being unwanted.' People in our society are crying out to belong, there are so many who are lonely and isolated, and are simply desperate for love.

You Don't Know Me

Having done a fair portion of my growing up in the late 1980s, I've got to admit that deep down I'm a bit of a soul boy. There's nothing quite like the chocolate tones of a soaring diva to get me feeling relaxed, and if I were to crown one of them queen, the honour would have to go to Whitney Houston. When I heard she was playing at Wembley Arena I arranged tickets as a surprise for my mate Gary's birthday. We shuffled gently and mouthed the words with her as she eased her way through classics like 'I'm every woman' and 'I will always love you'. It was a top night, made even more memorable by one exchange that took place as Ms H returned to the stage for her second set. A few rows behind me, a group of guys starting chanting, 'We love you, Whitney.'

'How can you love me?' she replied. 'You don't even know me.'

For those fans it probably wasn't the kind of reply they were looking for, but for me, the words rang in my ears for days on end. How can we love God when we don't know him? When we treat him like an entertainer – someone who is there to make us all feel warm and cuddly inside – but don't spend time with him, one on one, how can we be anything other than spectators?

The truth about love is that it needs fuel. Without spending time on the relationship, the 'I love you's and the occasional gifts are nothing more than hollow words and actions without substance. Put another way, if you don't stoke the fire, how can you expect a furnace?

Intimacy is to love what grapes are to wine – it is the raw ingredient that gets distilled over time to produce the final vintage. Without the commitment to spending regular quality time with God, then love will never get beyond the puppy phase. The Bible says that when we draw near to God he draws nears to us. Practically speaking we need to build space into our lives and diaries where we can sit and be with God, allowing him to speak to us and us to speak to him.

Do you believe in love at first sight? Ness once worked for me, and Nathan was my flatmate. When they first met they didn't fall in love at first sight; in fact, Ness didn't much like Nathan at all. When they eventually did get it together Nathan said, 'You don't fall in love, you grow in love.' How true that is. In the summer of 1999 their love grew to the point where they gave themselves to each other for the rest of their lives in marriage. Our intimate love with God is not something we fall into or is just handed to us. It is something that we grow into and give ourselves to develop.

When the New Testament focuses on the subject of relationship with God, it often does so using marriage as a metaphor. In it, the church is the bride and Christ is the groom. I don't know if he'll have a stag night, but the writers of the Bible often suggest that when Christ returns he will be reunited with his bride, their intimate union meaning an end to the imperfections of our lives and the universe. It's also interesting that the same Hebrew word (meaning 'to know') used in the Old

Testament to describe the way that God relates to his people is also used to describe the way that a husband and wife know each other. In the same way that man and wife become one through their shared intimacy, so too does God offer us the chance to share everything with him in an intimate relationship that – because of his very nature – goes beyond any human relationship.

The challenge of pursuing intimacy with God is always opposed by the many other attractions currently playing in our lives. Whether it's romance, ambition, entertainment or introspection, we need to be aware of the appetites that exist within us, especially those that are particularly adept at drawing us away from God. It's not wrong to have lots of interests, but it is impossible (as the Bible says) to be the slave of two masters. What's more, when we give in to the stronger urges, they almost always end up taking us further than we want to go. Instead, if we are serious about discovering the life we were created to lead we need to get the number one priority sorted first – an intimate relationship with God – and allow the other things to fall into line behind and beneath it.

It seems strange to write this, but there are definite signs that this intimacy thing is catching on. We're all used to hearing cultural analysts portray the current climate as being characterised by a hard-nosed, everyone-for-themself attitude. In truth, though, recent years have brought with them an increasing appreciation of the otherness of life. For years science has been god, dictating that unless something could be explained, dissected and put neatly into a pie chart, then it could not be real. Logic and rationality stepped up to the microphone and started cussing miracles, spirituality and anything that didn't fit into their prescribed parameters. Now, though, it's clear to see that we've left that culture, and have entered a new one, where interest in mystery, the supernatural and things beyond our Ken (whoever Ken may be) are firmly on the menu. Take a trip into any bookshop, and in the religious section you'll find evidence that holds this claim up. You might find a few tomes on Christianity and world religions, but for every one of them you'll be sure to find a handful of volumes on New Ageism and alternative spirituality. Suddenly, there's a great interest in things that we don't have answers for.

So where does that leave you and me? Do we hide under the duvet of doubt, quivering in case someone discovers us as impostors in the religious dormitory? Of course not. What we can do is play on the themes that are common to all. After all, being able to have a full on relationship with the Creator of the entire universe – an unseen yet all-powerful force – is a bit of a trip. Let's use it, joining the others in the spirit of exploration and experience.

Movies in 1998 didn't get much bigger than multiple-Oscar winner *Titanic*. The budget was huge, the set immense and the box office receipts astronomical. In keeping with this sense of size was the central theme;

that most universal of needs – love. The message that was left bobbing on the surface was that love costs. Jack Dawson ended up handing over his life for love but, along the way, Rose was prepared to give up her prosperity-bound future as well as her own life as a response to the passions of her heart.

So, we've sussed out that love is powerful. Without it, we end up being abrasive, curt and missing the point of life. When we have it, we have the power to change things – even the most desperate of situations. We also know that love comes with a price – it might mean anything from making a few comfort-depriving sacrifices to surrendering our last breath. There might not be many of us who, at the last minute, would actually die for something or someone else, and there will be even fewer of us who will have to carry it through. However, when it comes to sacrificial love, the key is not just reaching the destination, but travelling in the right direction; not holding out for one huge act of sacrifice, but practising daily in smaller and less dramatic situations.

According to contemporary culture, this is a load of rubbish. Ever since James Dean took that fatal ride we've been bowing down at the altar of 'Live fast, die young'. We may not all have been going supernova like Jim Morrison or soaking it all up like George Best, but we have followed their lead in certain, less dramatic ways. Love has become easy, cheap and neatly packaged. We impose the rules of channel surfing on affairs of the heart, switching over to something else if things get boring or too much like hard work.

To discover your destiny is to know that you are born for a relationship of intimacy with God which may cost you everything, but that is the nature of the lover.

Action

1 In what ways do you seek intimacy with God? What practical things could you try, to work at that intimacy with him?

2 What are some of the appetites you have that can draw your love and attentions away from God? Pray and declare to God that he is your greatest love.

3 With a friend, talk about some of the sacrifices you have made in recent years in making your relationship with God your priority. Write down the sacrifices that you anticipate having to make as you continue to love God.

4 Imagine you had just met God down the pub. What are some of the first conversations you would have with him? As you get to know him how would you express your commitment and love to him?

3

The Authenticator

Today is not a good day. Not only am I tired and emotional, but I have on my conscience a triple bill of social crimes: death, wastage and the annoyance of a person in authority. I will be punished, but not quickly. People will point and stare as I go about the business of rebuilding my shattered life. A pariah, I will be confined to life on the fringes of civilisation, locked out with all the other undesirables – the estate agents, the double-glazing salespeople and the bloke responsible for Mr Blobby. I can see this torment extending into the distance like a ship crawling towards the horizon. Sure, the pain may subside, but right now I'm convinced that my tomb will bear the words, 'Here lies Matt Bird: killer of goldfish, defroster of freezers and enemy of caretakers'. All those things I had hoped to achieve will be forgotten or failed.

Alone now, I face the saddest truth of all: there is nothing so painful as the death of a dream.

It started last night. This is 1993 and I'm training to be a vicar in Birmingham. My home is a hall of residence just south of the city centre, owned by the college. There are over fifty of us living here in an early Victorian building that was constructed to house nuns. The main hall, with its high ceiling, gallery and floor like an ice rink is one of those places that just begs to be rammed every Friday night with parties. And so we do, but when we don't we rent it out to other people for them to use for parties and functions. This all works pretty well, and bar the odd bit of puke on the begonias, problems have never seemed to arise.

Until last night. I'd been out and returned at 1.30 a.m. A dull but persistent thud greeted me as I pulled into the driveway and by the time I'd made it upstairs to my room the persistence hadn't changed much but the dull thud had become more of a nightmarish subterranean explosion. Like hostages on the eighty-fourth day, my fellow residents were walking about the corridors, stunned and weary. Parties were supposed to end at midnight, but no one had thought to go down and remind the selection of merrymakers from the Irish Social Club's Rugby XV.

Fired on by a desire to get to my bed as soon as possible I strode down to the hall, went to the back and helped myself to a substantial decrease in volume. With a polite smile I explained that things needed to finish as this was our home and we all wanted to get some sleep. As I walked out I was kind of surprised that a few of them hadn't taken my words seriously and was intrigued as to why it should make them question the legitimacy of my birth. Still, the music was off and the pillow beckoned. Result.

Fifteen minutes later the tunes were back. It's amazing how influential the sound of Oirish Rebels can be when you're drifting in and out of sleep. I suddenly awoke from a dream where my head was being placed in a vice by giant leprechauns, each with identical bald head and ginger beard, just like the one in *The Simpsons*. I felt sick.

Swinging out of bed and into my oversized Dumbo slippers, I prepared for battle. I headed for the cellar, where I located the power switch and moved it gently from 'on' to 'off'. Chuckling to myself I returned to my room in the dark. While there still wasn't total silence, I found the noise of the organisers swearing as they cleared up in the dark to be infinitely more appealing than their techno version of 'When Irish eyes are smiling'.

You'll understand then, that I woke up this morning feeling pretty good about things. As I trotted over to the main building to pick up my post I bumped into the caretaker. Looking slightly worn out himself, I decided to let him know that it was I he should thank for the little sleep that he did get last night. After a blow-by-blow account – pausing only for dramatic effect and to allow myself time to create a handful of choice embellishments – I stepped back and waited for his congratulations.

They didn't come. Instead I was informed that he was just returning from the principal's house. It seems that there had been some problem with his freezer during the night, and he had been greeted in the morning by a pool of water covering the kitchen floor and a lukewarm freezer containing steaks and pies that were rapidly approaching nauseating levels of rancidity. This had added to the caretaker's sense of confusion as he too had woken up to find mysterious circumstances awaiting him downstairs. His prized collection of tropical fish, the ones whose life and death was placed in the hands of an electronic pump, had mysteriously died in the early hours of the morning. My information allowed him to piece the whole jigsaw together, and through the mixture of tears and fuming anger, he slowly explained to me that the whole site – including the main hall, principal's house and caretaker's lodge – was on a single power circuit.

With the benefit of a few hours' breathing space, I think our early morning meeting went quite well. Yes it may have been slightly unusual to have been chased around the main quad by an irate sixty-year-old, and it certainly proved that he is far fitter than his age would suggest. Still, I'm sure his decision to have a scaffolding pipe in his right hand slowed him down to the point where my escape was guaranteed.

We've all been there, we've all messed up big time or that's the way it feels when we are in the middle of it.

Somewhere along the way, life seems to get full of mistakes. No matter how many 'be good's, 'eat healthily's and 'work hard's we put down on our list, the basket always seems to fill up with an astounding variety of glitches and system errors. From snapped one-liners to years of neglect, each of us has an ability to develop a catalogue of let-downs that would embarrass even the most humble of TV evangelists.

I travel a lot, and often if I'm going to be flying I'll have to get up at a ridiculously early hour in the morning. On one occasion I had to be up at 4 a.m., which meant sorting myself out with a serious wake-up call. As someone who gets through alarm clocks on a reasonably regular basis – either by breaking them or becoming immune to their noises – I was interested when a friend had recently been waxing lyrical about the greatness of his latest addition to his hi-fi. It was a radio tuner that had a built-in clock and the ability to get all the other bits of hi-fi working at a desired time. I decided that this was the way forward, and made my way to the nearest shop where I could spend a couple of hours browsing. I came out with the very latest in anti-sleep technology: a tuner with built-in alarm and full cascading capabilities. In other words, the longer I ignored it, the louder it got. Genius.

It worked. I was up at four, out the door by 4.36 a.m. and in the air by 7.00 a.m. When I returned a week later, I was greeted by a handwritten letter from the lady in the flat above. It gently informed me that she too had been aware of my latest purchase, as it had continued to kick in every morning at the same time while I was away. The cascade function had ensured that within minutes the volume was high enough to rouse her from her sleep, continuing to rise for at least another twenty minutes, by which time it was just about beginning to get light. While she appreciated knowing the relevant issues affecting farming today, she felt sure that she would rather gather the information at a more sociable time. I felt terrible. I went round as soon as I could with a card and chocolates in an attempt to make it up to her. I promised that I would make sure it would never happen again.

The trouble with 4 a.m. is that logical thought and memory go out of the window. If I've got to get up that early then the chances are that once I'm up, I'll be thinking about nothing other than the fact I've got so many minutes left before I have to be out of the flat. Remembering to reset my cascading alarm is not the first thing on my mind, or at least it wasn't when I used it to get me up early for another trip a month later. I immediately recognised the handwriting on the note that greeted me on my return. It had happened again. I decided to find another alarm clock.

You Are How You Hurt

The way that we behave authenticates what we believe. If I claim to be a saint at the same time as exploiting others, then my saintliness doesn't really exist and I have no right to go on about it. Likewise, if I claim to be a true hedonist and spend my time bombed out of my mind, then my words — if not my lifestyle — do at least have some truth about them. At the extreme you can call it hypocrisy, but the lack of integrity that shrouds so many lives these days is a deeply unattractive trait. Discovering your destiny means making sure that your words are backed up by your deeds. It means being an authenticator.

We all know what it's like to have someone at work turn round to us and deliver the stab of 'and you call yourself a Christian'. So many times we let God, ourselves and others down, and when we do the chances are that there will be others on hand to notice. Of course we can't expect to be perfect, nor am I suggesting that we all become expert in hiding our sin and putting up a smokescreen to the watching world. It's a huge challenge, but one we all must face up to. We will never be without mistakes, but we can try and whittle them down at the same time as pursuing integrity as fully as possible.

Being a bloke there are one or two areas in which I struggle to match up my words with my deeds, particularly when I'm driving in the fast lane of the M25. A car comes up behind and flashes his lights, telling me to shift over into the next lane. I won't. I'm already a fraction over the speed limit, but Matey Boy behind wants to push it even faster. Shifting to the left means getting snarled up by some nasty looking caravans and cruisers which is, of course, unacceptable. So I stay precisely where I am, for a while. The flashing increases, the image in my rear-view mirror gets bigger as he pulls even closer to me. I can almost see his bulging veins as his head and neck squeeze out of his shirt like a beetroot through a hosepipe. He doesn't like me. Tough. I was here first.

Finally the adrenaline gets overtaken by common sense and I move over, but not without gaining one more momentous victory as I make my move from lane to lane about as slow as is humanly possible. I am in control. I am the winner. I am the man.

But then he's passed me and I'm back in my place – a slower driver in a weaker car. His passing is his opportunity for revenge; mouthing words that are easily lip-read, offering hand signals that are about as subtle as they are imaginative. He speeds away and I have lost.

Driving around London I'm constantly challenged on this one. How can I make sure that my actions measure up to my words? How can I be authentic in my life? It's fine to be full of principles, but unless we put them into practice, our chat and beliefs are a waste of space.

One year a group of us decided to go skiing in the French Alps. We drove there and having survived the twelve-hour journey we arrived feeling suitably tired, but also as happy and united as any bunch of mates could wish to be. The days were a spectacular mixture of fresh snow, inspiring views and exhilarating skiing. Come the evening we were all knackered and took it in turns to cook.

Back in England someone had had an idea about spending the rest of the evenings playing games like Risk. It was a mistake. After just two attempts, our collective sense of harmony, peace and love had mutated into blind ambition, hatred and very real threats of violence. Risk is about world domination, and it is surely the most destructive game ever to have been cynically marketed as entertainment. Playing it brought out the worst in our characters: the competitiveness and inability to accept defeat. All it took was little bit of encouragement, and we were in serious danger of blowing all our authenticity as friends in one round of WWIII.

I went on a 'Wines of the World' course once, and over the five weeks I found out more than I thought possible about my favourite drink. Not only did we get to sample some fantastic wines and learn how to tell them apart from vinegar, but we also got to look at the bottles. OK, so this might not sound like much in the way of excitement to you but to me it was a real eye-opener. Some of the wines that came in ornate and exquisite bottles were real let-downs, while tipples like the Hunter Valley Brokenback Shiraz may not have counted for much on the outside, but once they were out of the drab-looking bottles, they were fantastic. As authenticators, our outside needs to be consistent with our inside; the private areas of our life consistent with our public life.

I saw a piece of pretentious editorial on Tupperware once. It said that 'for postmodern cuisine it's not content but the form that's of the essence, not the vitals but the vessel, if you like. So the re-emergence of Tupperware as top of the pots comes as no surprise.' For us Christians it is not simply enough to say that the container looks good – we have to ask about the contents. Image is not everything; internal integrity that validates all we do is the most vital ingredient for all our lives.

In our postmodern society there's an almost universal shrugging off of moral absolutes. Right and wrong seem about as culturally relevant as prawn cocktail and Danny La Rue. We've managed to sweep these two old boys under the carpet – right and wrong that is, not prawns and the cross-dressing entertainer – justifying the shift of the goalposts as progress. After all, who wants to live under the intolerant oppression of right and wrong? Who wants to be dictated to by Big Brother? We're amazing, so the advert tells us. We are all free, enlightened and unique beings, each one of us capable of finding the God within us, but never overstepping the boundaries by trying to impose our beliefs on someone else.

What should this mean to Christians? The Bible says that 'where there is no revelation the people cast off restraint', and that is precisely what's going on around us today. There is no revelation of God – no comprehension of his holiness or personality – and people are casting off the restraint of moral absolutes. Behaviour and relationships have taken on a whole new tone, governed by the laws of post-modernity. Of course, in such an environment it's hard to pin post-modernity down with definitions. This makes things tricky for us. When we talk about living a righteous and authentic life, what do we measure it against? There is some hope, for while holiness has been packed up and placed in storage, integrity has managed to keep its place as one of the more popular virtues. At its most basic, integrity is the act of practising what you preach. This trend is particularly apparent when you look at our reaction to sleazy politicians. You could spend the rest of this book compiling a list of all those who have fallen foul of public opinion through the uncovering of deeds which have undermined their words. Heck, just last week some poor old Tory got carted off to prison for perjury.

I remember hearing a story about Billy Graham who was preaching to a group of churchgoers one day. In the congregation was a young chap who was convinced that when it came to preaching he could kick the old man's butt. Trying hard to conceal his ambition, he sauntered up to Billy at the end of the meeting and asked him how his ministry had done so well, especially when one considered the numerous other preachers around who could also kick his butt. Billy graciously informed the young punk of one of life's deepest truths. 'Because,' he said, 'I've lived the life of an evangelist for the last five decades.' You see, it's all about integrity, and our Bill had been walking the walk long enough for his words to have the deep ring of authenticity. Anyone in a position of influence, leadership or management needs integrity.

Influence demands it, and it simply will not take second best.

American Christian Jimmy Bakker's autobiography *I Was Wrong* is a fascinating story of the life of a man who made a mistake. Not only did he set up a Christian TV station and the Heritage USA theme park, but his influence reached far across the country, making him a thoroughly respected man. The book details how all this was thrown away when he spent fifteen minutes in a hotel room with a woman who wasn't his wife, just to make Mrs Bakker jealous and to get her attention. That single act of infidelity was the catalyst for the destruction of all that he had achieved up until then. It is true that the greater the influence that we have, the greater the integrity we need to have in place. The greater the influence we have, the greater the trust people will place in us, and if that trust is shattered the damage is widespread and highly destructive. If we miss out on this vital truth, we fail to authenticate everything that we claim our lives to be about.

The Whole Truth

I love the film *Jerry Maguire*. It was one of the most moral films of 1997, and managed to deliver a message bound up with an unusual amount of positive influence. As an agent for some of the world's top athletes, Maguire works in the heart of a cut-throat business community. He's lean and mean, until one night he sits up and watches as he spews a memo that highlights the lack of good values in his work. Suddenly aware of the lack of integrity surrounding the industry, he suggests taking on fewer clients, earning less money and giving a more personal service. He gets the sack.

Jerry Maguire found out that integrity is the secret ingredient needed in every business. It might not bring success, to some it might not even make decent business sense, but the truth is welded into place for you and me to discover. With integrity at the heart of his business, Jerry's new company takes a long time to pick up – and even at the end there are no guarantees that he is ever going to approach the heights previously scaled. But his company is value-based, it is ethical and it has authenticity. Whatever we do must carry that same commitment to honesty. It must be the lifeblood that feeds our every decision. Will you be prepared to lose out for the sake of the truth – even to the point of redundancy?

A friend of mine – James – has been very successful in the marketing world. His suits are crisp, his manner personable and efficient and his life is a success. He has worked hard and been rewarded well. But it isn't always easy. He deals with a bewildering array of multinational corporations, the sort where the pound is king and to be pursued at any price. He was recently working with one particular company when he found out that there was some underhand money being passed around. James happened to be making a packet out of the company in question, but he faced a choice. Either he kept his gob shut and carried on counting the cash, or he blew the whistle on them, risking not only the loss of their cash but their considerable wrath. He opted for integrity. He lost the contract.

When I was a student in Birmingham I used to go down Harborne High Street each week to do my shopping. One day I saw a couple of guys collecting money and giving out badges. Like most of us I quickened my pace and hurried past them, pretending to be late/deep in thought/troubled/potentially dangerous. It was only when I had done my shopping and I saw them again that I started to wonder. Something didn't seem quite right so I went up for a chat.

'Who are you collecting for?' I asked.

'We are collecting for needy children,' replied one.

'Yes,' said the other. 'Needy children.'

'Oh?' I replied. 'What's the name of the charity?'

'It's the Needy Children Charity,' replied number one.

'Yes,' said the other. 'Needy children.'

Something definitely didn't seem right so, having chatted with them for a while longer, I asked to see their ID and copied down the telephone number printed on it. I told them that I was up for giving them some cash, but that I wanted just to check it out first. As I made my way to the phone box, they started shouting at me before running away. Sure enough, they were crooks – either that or the Needy Children Charity did a lot of work through Mr Wu's Chinese Express. I felt saddened by this reminder of the amount of injustice that thrives in the world.

It was very interesting that after the 1997 general election, on their first day in power, the new government were gathered by their leader and given the following talk. 'We are here to work,' said Tony Blair, 'not to enjoy the trappings of power. We need discipline, unity and co-ordination. There is hope and optimism out there, but there is a lot of hard work to be done in here.'

One of the greatest characteristics that authenticates leadership is servanthood. It's not about seeking after status, recognition and all those other 'trappings of power', but getting on with the job as best you can.

In this age of talent shows, hand-picked boy and girl bands and the celebrity culture, it's not surprising that a tangible portion of the population suffers from a condition known as Pushy Mother Syndrome. Symptoms include the almost ruthless determination for the child to succeed, an inability to accept any form of criticism about their offspring (except, of course, that which they think of themselves) and a total absence of any form of embarrassment at the lengths they will go to in achieving their dream. But this is not a new phenomenon, as it is well documented in God's book.

The mother in question takes her two boys, James and John, to see Jesus with a request that would impress even the most accomplished of PMs. Instead of asking for a decent warm-up slot at one of the next preaching gigs or suggesting that her two might be well worth considering for a special mention in one of his stories, she has the audacity to ask Jesus if he wouldn't mind granting her two lovely lads the honour of sitting either side of him in heaven for all eternity. The other disciples find out and are understandably incensed that such a blatant request for the highest honour should be made. Mum is, we must assume, totally indignant and defends her request to the bitter end.

Jesus's reaction is simple yet profound. Instead of getting involved in her negotiations he rewrites the rule book on the spot. 'Whoever wants to become great among you must be your servant, and whoever wants to be first must be slave of all.' Interestingly this doesn't suggest that to be a person of great power, authority and influence you need to start at the bottom and work your way up. It actually says that authentic leadership is servant leadership. There is no promotion beyond servant leadership. 'For even,' Jesus concludes, 'the Son of Man didn't come to be served but to serve and to give his life as a ransom for many.'

Nothing has ever made me think about the servant nature of Jesus as much as a trip to Israel I was leading a while ago. As we stood at the top of the Mount of Olives, looking out across the city of Jerusalem, we remembered the way that God's people had continually ignored and fought against his prophets. We then walked down to the Garden of Gethsemane, where Jesus had prayed and the disciples failed to stay awake. We remembered his words – 'yet not my will, but yours be done' – and thought about the strength of character and love that it took to be able to say that knowing what was coming next. Then we travelled to Caiaphas' house where it is thought that Jesus spent the night before his crucifixion. As we went down to the bottom of the house to the single, isolated cell, praying and reading the Bible, we were overcome by the sense of desperation and isolation that Jesus must have felt that night. Jesus lived his life as a servant of others, and if ever I needed to have that underlined, seeing the places associated with the build-up to his death brought it home to me.

As Philippians 2 says, Jesus, 'who being in very nature God, did not consider equality with God something to be grasped, but made himself nothing, taking the very nature of a servant, being made in human likeness. And being found in appearance as a man, he humbled himself and became obedient to death – even death on a cross.'

The Sharpening Stone

I'm not alone in this – I know there are plenty of you out there who feel the same – but I struggle to live an authentic life. I've screwed up in other ways besides the lightly humorous ones which started this chapter. I believe that God works in our lives to make us more authentic, to help us live what we believe in. Don't get me wrong, I'm not suggesting that we trot along, puppet-like, responding to the controls of a malevolent master – slipping up on banana skins right on cue. No, I'm convinced that we are the sole credit-takers for our mistakes, but that God – in his infinite mercy and wisdom – can use them like a good hunter uses even the most extraneous of animal parts. What makes me think this? Let me tell you.

When I was twenty years old my dad phoned me at home one day. 'She's gone,' he said in a tone of shocked confusion. We had all been at his mother's funeral a couple of days before, and I assumed that this was another part in his grieving.

'I know she's gone, Dad,' I answered.

'No,' he said. 'It's your mum – that's who's gone.'

He told me that my mum had left him that morning. It was a difficult phone call. I too was shocked, but hurt and upset as well. I did what seemed like the obvious thing and phoned my prayer partner. He was a lot more mature than me, but midway through the conversation I realised that he wasn't just letting me speak, but he had gone silent on me. I waited. Then I realised.

Later the whole story came out. My mother and my prayer partner had been having an affair for a while. I was devastated. I felt totally betrayed and let down. It was a truly difficult time for me, and as I look back it stands out as one of the major crises of my life.

The truth is that this story doesn't get followed by a yawning 'but' followed by an explanation of how God has made it all right. It's not all right, it certainly wasn't OK, *and* God taught me something through it. It broke me, humbled me and through it God took hold of me and helped me along this part of my journey. I don't think it happened specifically so that God could give me a few tweaks here and there – that would make him sound altogether too dark and unpleasant – but I know he's used it.

A few years on in the story of my life I was to be found training to be a vicar in the church. It ended up not working out as I had hoped (and believe me, I'd had many hopes surrounding it). Eventually they refused to let me go forward to ordination and again, I found myself in the middle of another time that would go down on my life's map as a crisis.

While the splitting up of my parents hit all my panic buttons relating to security and belonging, this one landed a nuclear left-hook right at the heart of my belief in God. I had been so sure that ordination was what God had wanted me to do. It was the reason I left the Admiralty, and was the very best way that I thought I could serve God. But then I got dropped and everything was different. My head, as you can imagine, was spinning.

I was left with four responses. First, God hadn't really spoken. This one led on to a whole load of other tough questions like how then do you hear from God? How does he make his thoughts known? How on earth can you find out what he wants you to do with your life?

The second option was to declare that the church had simply got in the way of what God had wanted to do. OK, so this may have been partly true, but it had the added disadvantage of seeming a tad arrogant and unpleasantly self-righteous.

Number three was to write myself off as a failure and get totally down about it all. This meant removing the situation from any form of context and suspending whatever objective judgment I may have been able to make.

Finally there was the choice of slamming the whole thing as God teaching me a lesson. This had the edge of making God sound like some sickie, or a sadist who was in it for laughs. I must say that this didn't really square off with my understanding of God and his character.

These were the only responses I could come up with after many months of struggling to make sense of it. Even now I can find no other explanation for why the events took place. If I'm honest, I don't like any of them much, and I certainly haven't made camp in any one of them. What I do know is that through the whole experience I had to trust God without trite answers. I also became bluntly honest with him. It shaped me and broke me.

Soon after everything had come crashing down around me some mates bought me a plane ticket to LA and encouraged me to go away for a break. I stayed with a friend in California and returned two weeks later feeling a bit better about things. On my first morning there I came downstairs and sat in the lounge. After having done a bit of staring into space, I picked up a book and flicked to a chapter that jumped out at me as if God had written it directly for me. It tackled the theme of life-maturing experiences, and worked through the idea that it is the difficult things in life that make us who we are, rather than the easy ones. There are some lessons that God can only teach through direct experience. In other words, no matter how many seminars we sit in on or tapes we listen to, the most profound and long-lasting lessons that we will apply to our lives are those taught in the classroom of one, where pain and frustration are the teachers and we are the pupils.

God is constantly at work on our character and he often uses wounding experiences to shape us. There is a chain reaction that goes like this: suffering produces perseverance produces character produces hope. The trouble is, this philosophy can only really be preached once it has been experienced. That needn't be a cause for alarm, because we are all destined to encounter events and experiences that rock our world. The syllabus at the University of Life is remarkably uniform – the only difference will be how we choose to react. Some of us will opt for the door marked 'bitter', others will struggle towards the one marked 'better'.

My friend Jeff is one of those communicators whose observational humour is astounding. He says that most people treat bitterness like a cute puppy, holding it close and nurturing it in their arms. In fact bitterness is far more like acid, in time corroding anything that it comes into contact with, destroying life.

Job was a man who was righteous, faithful and – at the point where we meet him in the Bible – the recipient of some of the toughest suffering imaginable. Much like our friends gather round us when we're going through it, Job's buddies got together to give him the benefit of their own considerable wisdom. The trouble was their answers were seriously trite. They encouraged him to curse God and blame it all on him. Job didn't go quite that far – although he did actually curse the day he was born – instead he kept on with God, refusing to airbrush out the harsh realities of life.

Job hooked into a decent truth: sometimes crap does happen, and when it does the best thing to do is not to try and find out why, but to get down to the business of responding with an integrity that matches up to the words of strength, commitment and dedication we utter in moments of easy glory. Like Job, as well as like the urban drivers, we need to work on our reactions under pressure. It can be easy to be faithful, pleasant and good when everything is going swimmingly and the roads are clear. Chuck in a few tragedies and some boy racers in the next lane, and keeping your faith and your cool become slightly harder. 'If,' as Mr Kipling said, 'you can keep your head when all about you are losing theirs', if you can keep your faith when all about you are telling you to ditch it, then you'll be a true, bona fide and authentic Christian.

The prophet Amos said on behalf of God:

I hate, I despise your religious feasts, I cannot stand your assemblies. Even though you bring me burnt offerings and grain offerings I will not accept them.

Though you bring me choice fellowship offerings, I will have no regard for them. Away with the noise of your songs! I will not listen to the music of your harps. (Amos 5:21–2)

To me it sounds as though God's on a bit of a downer: no big meals, no festivals or conferences, no gifts and offerings, no cells and community, no songs or music – is this the God we know? Just as I'm about to panic, Amos chips in further, 'But let justice roll on like a river, righteousness like a never-failing stream' (Amos 5:24).

Christians never tell lies – we just sing them – and all that religious paraphernalia, the songs, music and hanging out together is worthless unless we are living a life that is focusing on God-flavoured justice and righteousness. What God is looking for within the depths of our character is a life of authentic reality, a life which behaves what it professes to believe. What point is faith without works? It is complete rubbish.

The destiny for true leaders is to live in a state of reality. There can be no future in ignoring pain and suffering and all their attendant questions. Our words must match our deeds, and the only way of learning that lesson is to go through periods when we really are taken up on those words. When I gave my life to God, I don't think I believed that he would begin to take me even remotely seriously. Through the mother and ordination experiences I can see that he has already asked me to put a few things on the line, but somewhere in the deep of my mind there is a sneaking feeling that he may well turn around and ask for more, much more – perhaps even as much as I promise him. I hope he does ask, and I hope my words ring true. I hope I can be more of an authenticator.

As this book was getting written, the world was shocked by the shootings in a high school in Denver, Colorado. Two boys shot fourteen of their fellow students, one of them being Cassie Barnall. She turned a corner and walked straight into one of the killers, who placed a gun at her head and asked her a simple question: do you believe in God? When she answered that she believed in Jesus Christ, at that moment she went to be with him.

Her example of the strength of character and faith that refuses to falter even in the face of death is relevant to us all. We need to be a generation that is equally authentic in the way that we live our lives. Why? Because that is how we were created to live.

Action

1 In what ways have you blown it in the last week? Pray and ask God's forgiveness.
2 What are the parts of your life in which you struggle for integrity? Ask a close friend to encourage you in those areas and give them permission to ask you regularly how you are getting on.
3 Have there been any crises in your life that remain full of hurt and unanswered questions? Have they

made you bitter or better? If bitter then get someone to pray with you quick.

4 How could you live your life so that it is more transparent and authentic? Perhaps sit down with a friend and work this one out together.

4

The Innovator

In today's paper, tucked away between a feature on unemployment and global recession, I found a great article. It made me smile so much that when my neighbour walked past my window she looked twice, the first time surprised to see me on the ledge, the second time concerned that I should be doing so with such a vacantly ecstatic look on my face. But it was worth the embarrassment, and I would encourage you too to get on your pyjamas right now and place yourself in full view of the watching world as you read on.

Larry Walters is among the relatively few who have actually turned their dreams into reality. His story is true, as hard as you may find it to believe . . . Walters was a truck driver, but his lifelong dream was to fly. When he graduated from high school, he joined the Air Force in the hope of becoming a pilot. Unfortunately, poor eyesight disqualified him, so when he finally left the service, he had to satisfy himself with watching others fly the fighter jets that criss-crossed the skies over his backyard. As he sat there in his lawn chair, he dreamed about the magic of flying.

Then one day, Walters had an idea. He went down to the local Army and Navy surplus store and bought forty-five weather balloons and several tanks of helium. These were not your brightly coloured party balloons; these were heavy-duty spheres measuring more than four feet across when fully inflated. Back in his yard, Walters used straps to attach the balloons to his lawn chair. He anchored the chair to the bumper of his jeep, and inflated the balloons with helium. Then he packed a few sandwiches and drinks, and a loaded air rifle, figuring he could pop a few balloons when it was time to return to Earth. His preparations complete, Walters sat in his chair and cut the anchoring cord. His plan was to lazily float into the sky, and eventually back to terra firma. But things didn't quite work out that way.

When Walters cut the cord, he didn't float lazily up; he shot up as if fired from a cannon. He didn't stop at thirty feet, and nor did he ease off once he reached fifty, or even one hundred. He climbed swiftly to one thousand feet, but still kept on going. Finally, he levelled off at eleven thousand feet. At that height, he couldn't risk deflating any of the balloons, lest he unbalance the load and really experience flying. So he stayed up there, sailing around for fourteen hours, totally at a loss about how to get down.

Eventually, Mr Walters drifted into the approach corridor for Los Angeles International Airport. A Pan Am pilot radioed the tower about passing a guy in a lawn chair at eleven thousand feet, with a gun in his lap. LAX is right on the ocean, and come nightfall, the winds on the coast begin to change. So, as dusk fell, Mr Walters began drifting out to sea. At that point, the Navy dispatched a helicopter to rescue him, but the rescue team had a hard time getting to him because the draught from their propeller kept pushing his home-made contraption farther and farther away.

Eventually, they were able to hover above him and drop a rescue line, with which they gradually hauled him back to safety. As soon as Mr Walters hit the ground, he was arrested. But as he was led away in handcuffs, a television reporter called out, 'Sir, why'd you do it?'

Mr Walters stopped, eyed the man, then replied nonchalantly, 'A man can't just sit around.'

The fun cost Mr Walters a total of US$1,000 in an out-of-court settlement with the aviation administration which said he operated too close to the airport, flew in a reckless manner and failed to maintain contact with the control tower. When asked, he said, 'I only did it because it was my lifelong dream to fly.'

History's roll-call is marked by the presence of dreamers. I'm not talking stoned-out wasters or reality-dodging fantasisers, but the type of full-on instigators who make a difference. Like Martin Luther King. He had a dream and gave his all to its fulfilment. Or William Wilberforce, who dreamt that slavery would be abolished. Bob Geldof wanted to do something to relieve the suffering in Ethiopia. Bill Gates wants to see a Windows-run PC in every home. Richard Branson wants to see the Virgin brand across as many products as possible.

Despite the fact that it has received high-profile support from anyone from princesses to footballers, the issue of landmines has been placed on the agenda for years by many unknown individuals. While they have quietly lobbied and applied pressure, significant advances have been made, among them the signing of the Ottawa Treaty in 1997. No fewer than 123 countries signed up for a ban on future use of anti-personnel landmines, and I am convinced that this step forward was made possible by both the public and the private acts of people concerned about this pro-life issue. Sometimes, people who end up instigating great change never receive recognition but again, this humility is a by-product of the integrity at the heart of the innovator.

We all know what it's like to be frustrated with something, and some of the time we even end up feeling frustrated by our frustrations. But whatever the cause – be it society, politics, relationships, oppression – I believe that frustration is our friend, and should be welcomed as one of the primary sources of motivation to see things changed. By their very nature, innovators will always be frustrated by certain situations; they are not content to sit back and allow things to carry on poorly.

While I may question the ultimate cause, I admire the commitment, tenacity and effectiveness of the gay pressure group OutRage! Thirty years ago homosexuality was socially unacceptable and considered by the majority of the population to be only slightly above terrorism in their list of 'Things We Don't Like'. OutRage! formed and decided to put an end to the inequality. Today, while discrimination and hatred exists, they have been marginalised and adopted by the lunatic fringe. Homosexuality has gone against the flow. Homosexual practices between consenting adults became legal in 1967 and have increasingly become an established and accepted way of life. Gay holidays, magazines and pubs now seem no more unusual than the Christian ones, and landmark events like the lowering of the age of consent seem to have an air of inevitability about them. Surely the credit for much of this must lie at the feet of an initially small band of radicals who committed themselves to do all they could to see the fulfilling of their dream.

Dream Small: Live Small

I think that we tend to dream fairly small-time. Job, car, house, holidays, relationship – having settled into our twenties most of us would place these reasonably high on our list of aims. Ten or fifteen years further down the line and these mutate into a list made up of: promotion, security, house, comfort, provision for family, provision for retirement. Scary, huh?

You may think that the chances of you worrying about retirement and so on are about as likely as you ever wanting an anti-slip bath mat, but they creep up on you. One thing leads to another and a logical progression takes place. Not that there's anything wrong with holidays, jobs, families and responsibility – they can all be wonderful things – but placing them as the main events in life, increasing their importance, scales down our dreams.

We Western Christians like to place our dreams within a reasonably small box. We opt for tens instead of thousands, church instead of politics and present-inspired caution instead of reckless future dreams. It hasn't always been this way though; a few radicals have always managed to slip through the net and try to keep the rest of us on our toes. There was a time, however, when that type of instigator was not in the minority. Jesus kick-started the whole thing by proving himself to be the most radical man that ever lived. He turned the established order of things upside down, promoting a new and improved way of living. The early Christians took up the challenge and continued to bury the dynamite of the gospel in the very foundations of civilisation. They chose not just to preach the gospel at selected sermons, but to adopt it as script for their lives. They fed the poor, lived in community, suffered at the hands of their enemies and stood up to be counted. They broke out of the legacy of the small box handed down to them by four hundred years of Israelite apathy and complacency. Not only did they challenge the national religion, but they broke out of a couple of thousand years of insularity by taking the new message out beyond the Israelites. Peter took it to Africa, Paul took it to Rome. With a crew of dangerous roughnecks in place, the dream remained large.

Some friends of mine, Chris and Kay, started their own business a few years ago with the aim of doing something that gave maximum credit to God. They had plans and dreams of what they might achieve, and through some serious hard work and some amazingly close shaves with bankruptcy, the reality of the business today has totally broken out of the box. The UK company has attracted significant venture capital funding and has moved from success to success. At the time of writing the power of God to blow our imagination out of the water is being brought home to them as they face moving to America for twelve months to establish their business there in a significant way. This is a massive step for the whole family to take because – apart from Chris – none has ever been to America. God has taken them up on their prayers that they might be able to make a big difference for him.

There's another friend I have called Simon who has unashamedly set out to earn as much money as possible so that he can give it away. Each year he and his wife pray about how much they should live on for the following twelve months, and as they feel God directs them they set a limit to the amount of cash they can keep for themselves for the rest of the year. Sometimes that is proportionately very small, but at others it is slightly more. Either way, whatever they earn over and above their limit goes into a trust fund that is used to finance kingdom-orientated ministries.

Innovators need to take the lid off the box. It is very easy to dream within the safe parameters of Christendom but we need to break out and think out of the box which is the nature of the kingdom of God. To put it another way, we need to take the ceiling off our small Christian world and to learn instead to dream big, huge, enormous and awesome ideas. As Paul declares to the believers at Ephesus, 'Now to him who is able to do immeasurably more than we ask or imagine, according to his power at work within us', God, we pray that you might do it in us. Isaiah prophesies in a similar vein; 'Enlarge the place of your tent, stretch your tent curtains wide, do not hold back; lengthen your cords, strengthen your stakes.'

Of course, having dreams is easy. We've all had them – some slightly more honourable than others (I can remember spending my entire thirteenth year thinking about nothing other than getting my hands on a Porsche 911) – but what makes the Martin Luther Kings, William Wilberforces, Pauls and Peters so special is the fact that they delivered. From inception right the way through to reality, they possessed the necessary faith and orientation towards action to see their plans come into being. And so we stumble across the single most important fact about nailing the innovator bit of our destiny; we must be able to complete. This doesn't mean being nightmarish control freaks incapable of letting go, believing that delegation is tantamount to castration. No, these people are the best leaders – the ones who recognise skills in others, who are able to trust, empower, and draw the best out of others. History may only recall the big names, but behind each of them were people built together in teams. To be an innovator therefore, you must be able to dream and deliver.

Actually, total delivery is something that will probably never happen in this life, for if you think back to Wilberforce, King and Geldof, there is more than one thing that they have in common. While they all had an idea of where they wanted to get to, very few actually saw reality totally correspond to their dreams. America is still infected with racism, the world of slavery continues behind closed doors and Sir Bob's help still couldn't prevent tragedy from striking Sierra Leone or countless other countries. The whole point of being a dreamer is to work towards a goal. It may never be fully reached – maybe not in one lifetime – but it's not necessarily about just reaching the destination, more about motion towards. No one can deny the progress that each of these leaders has made towards their dream.

Now we've got that straight there's a good chance that you're rapidly going off this whole leadership thing. After all, you've got to be committed as well as creative as well as inventive as well as gracious as well as authentic. Perhaps it would be easier to pack up now and go back and think about finance deals on a Volvo.

The Learning Curve

When I started Joshua Generation, I didn't have much of a clue. If you'd asked me about the end result I wanted to achieve I would have mumbled something about people and leadership, and if you'd asked me how it was going to happen I probably would have laughed nervously and tried to change the subject. This state of living for something without having much of a clue of how it will work out was a most valuable time, as my focus was kept small while the idea seemed to formulate around me.

My idea was simple (and I thought it was good). A lot of my friends were leaving university, drifting away from God, getting jobs and feeling as though there was absolutely no relationship between what little faith they did have and the pressures of life in a suit. In the process of finding work, many of them had moved to new areas and had for themselves a whole manner of troubles on their doorstep. Not only did they have the imminent crisis of finding accommodation; they had to make new friends and build a life sometimes from scratch. As church seemed to be increasingly irrelevant to many of them, so they constructed their universe without it.

As I saw this pattern begin to emerge, I wondered whether there was anything that could be done about it, anything that could help to reintegrate faith and an emerging adult life. I gathered a group of people for what I called a Young Leaders Weekend in the hope that together we might rediscover the glue that would hold these vital components together.

Out of that one weekend Joshua Generation was born. Of course, as time has gone on it has become clear that things started out being relatively, um, unclear. It has taken time to develop, but hopefully, like the people we're trying to work with, it will emerge and achieve its full potential in time.

However, since birth, the progress of Joshua Generation has taught some pretty decent lessons, and has gone through some very distinct stages. Looking back on each of our projects I'm sure I can see seven separate phases of growth, each one vital to the success of the next. What's more, having talked with others and done a bit of digging around, I'm sure that this model is one that can be applied to the growth of any plan. Here goes:

The first thing that needs to happen is the dream. It is vital that you allow God to give you the idea. God loves doing this, and has promised that the Holy Spirit would play a big part in the delivery of inspirations and ideas. After all, as the most creative entity in the universe, I would think it fair to say that God is fairly into letting the imagination have a little slack.

Once you've dreamed an idea, it can be hard to give it life. Too often we can leave it languishing in fantasy land, unable to rise beyond an indefinable sense of excitement. This is the time to conceptualise it – to imagine it actually taking place. Think about how your dream may happen, as well as when, where and with whom. Try to picture the whole thing taking off, and how you will get to that point.

Next up it's time for chat. This is vitally important for three reasons: first, because in telling people about what you want to do you road-test the idea itself and you clarify some of the details that may have escaped you so far; second, you will start to develop a sense of ownership of the thing from other people. Also, if you start getting the odd knock-back right now it will help get you in shape for the other obstacles which doubtless will follow in time.

Once that's begun it will be time to develop the idea. This means getting down to the business of the business. We're talking strategies, business plans, timetables, whatever you can to get things as focused as possible. At this stage of progress you're bound to come up against obstacles and problems. Some you'll have to work around, but others may well send you back a couple of stages so that you can tweak your idea to accommodate the necessary changes. It doesn't mean that yours was a dud in the first place, simply that it's getting closer to reality.

So what next? Try resourcing it. Hopefully with a good dose of the previous development under your belt this should be made slightly easier, as people see that your plan is to be taken seriously. Of the tangibles you'll need finance, time and space, but there will also be a need for real commitment from others. Try going back to all those people you talked to before and seeing if they'll be willing to be involved and continue owning the thing with you.

Once all that preparation is done it is finally time to deliver the idea. This means finally doing it, seeing what has taken all this time eventually come to life.

It's not over yet, though, as a vital part of realising any dream is continued evaluation. As any project grows, the way it is run will have to change alongside it. What's more, even if things are not growing particularly fast, evaluation remains an essential part of keeping things together; the longer you're running, the more you will learn. Without space to adapt – both to your increasing knowledge or the changing surroundings – there is a danger that all the hard work put into making a dream become reality could be wasted.

Each of us is able to dream. We were made in the image of God, whose own love of creation screams from every page in the Bible. Our inherited love of creation has encouraged us to place great importance on those whose own creative powers mark them out from the rest of us. The arts form the basis for much of this harvesting of talent, and many of the key players often have illuminating insights into the nature of creativity. Legendary rock *uber-meister* Keith Richards has been quoted as saying that 'all the great tunes are already out there. The secret is knowing how to pluck them out of the air.'

Paul McCartney managed to get a few more words out on the subject in his autobiography.

I always liken song writing to a conjuror pulling a rabbit out of a hat. Now you see it now you don't. If I now pick up a guitar and start to conjure something out of the air, there's a magic about it. Where there was nothing, now there is something. Where there was a sheet of paper, there's a page we can read. Where there was no tune and no lyrics, there's now a song we can sing . . . That creative moment when you come up with an idea is the greatest, it's the best. It's like sex. You're filled with a knowledge that you're right, which, when much of life is filled with guilt and the knowledge you are probably not right, is a magic moment. You actually are convinced it's right, and it's a very warm feeling that comes from the spine, through the cranium and out of the mouth.

We might not all be able to create music, but each of us needs to respond to the primal urges of creativity within. Being an innovator – responding to the dreams that lie within us all – is to be creative and to collect on the inheritance delivered to us at our birth.

As Christians we believe in a Creator God – one whose fingerprints are to be found all over the universe – who also chose to create men and women to be spiced with the flavours of his character. That means that we share his genes and step up to the microphone as co-creators, equally endowed with the need and ability to follow suit. Unfortunately our innate creativity has been damaged and damped by our own sloppiness and rebellion against him but thankfully, when we come back to God and receive the Holy Spirit into our lives, that creativity gets a decent once-over, ready once more to be unleashed to recreate the world in which we live to make it better.

The Legacy Lives On

Alfred Nobel enjoys a rather notable entry in fame's journals. He invented nitroglycerine and dynamite, and enjoyed more than fifteen minutes of fame as people around him celebrated his invaluable scientific advance. One day, while reading his daily paper, he chanced upon his own obituary. Having satisfied himself that he was in fact alive, and that this was not some bizarre celestial ritual to guide spirits through purgatory, Nobel read on. He later found out that there had been some confusion as it was a different Mr A Nobel who had died, but not before the reading of his obituary had made a profound impact on his life. As he read through it there was one main achievement that dominated all the others. Nobel was shocked to see his life summed up in terms of advances in weaponry and destruction. He stood face to face with his legacy and he did not like what he saw. At that point he decided to change direction, pouring his massive financial resources into setting up an annual prize to celebrate peace. His legacy of the Nobel prizes remains with us today, and it has been altered beyond all recognition from that which he read when he was alive.

Nobel is a great example to all of us, as we all should ask ourselves exactly what sort of legacy it is that we will be leaving once we've died. OK, so it may sound a tad morbid, but sometimes we need to weigh things up like this to gain a better perspective on the terrain of our life. Are we creating things that will leave a legacy of which we can be proud, or have we been producing something that, ultimately, we do not want to put our name to?

Driving back from my friends' place one night I saw some lights come down from the sky and land in a field. Surprised, I slowed down and took a closer look. Actually, a driver had lost control of his car and flipped off an embankment. I pulled over, dialled 999 and ran down towards the car that was crumpled upside down around a tree. I got the bloke out and sat him down away from the car, amazed that he had only suffered one small cut to his head. He was obviously stunned, both because of the accident and due to the fact that he was still alive. It was Christmas time, and I suggested that this Christmas he definitely had something to thank God for. Driving away later on, I was struck by the fragile nature of life. Things could have been so very different for that man, and by the time I had arrived he may have known his fate for all eternity. We like to think that we are immortal, but death can be cruelly sudden. I remembered a friend, Dennis, who was a Pentecostal minister in Northern Ireland. Within weeks of the doctors seeking a diagnosis, he was dead. He was forty-six. Whether our life is going to be taken from us swiftly or with warning, whether we will die from natural causes or external forces, we need to think about what our legacy will be. Perhaps the time to start thinking is now.

This quandary cannot be avoided by a shrug of the shoulders and a nonchalant cry of 'Oh, well, I suppose I won't leave a legacy at all, then'. Sorry, but that's just not an option. As soon as we're born we are up on the scoreboard, and our deeds are counting. You can no more opt out of leaving a legacy than you can being a witness for Christianity – as a Christian everything you do is automatically an example to the watching world. Our lives give evidence for or against the credibility of Christianity. It is not something that can be turned on and off at will, for Christianity is open 24 hours a day, 365 days of the year. Leaders who are innovators must think carefully about the sort of legacy that they want to leave – apathy and neglect offer no guarantee of success.

Nike's famous 'Just do it' advertising slogan could have been used equally well on Christians as on armchair sportspeople. We tend to be so poor at getting on with things, favouring a seemingly endless run of ponderings and wonderings about what the will of God may or may not be, hoping that he'll eventually write it in the sky and make it all nice and easy again. Of course, when we're innovating we need to be sensible and think through what lies ahead, but once that is done, there should be no excuse for paralysis and lethargy.

We need to apply what I describe as the Gamaliel principle, as it reminds me of what went on with the apostles and members of the early church. Havoc surrounded them as God began to move in the Jewish community, and they were hauled up before the Sanhedrin and warned never again to speak the name of Jesus. Peter laid it on the line by telling the bigwigs that the apostles had to obey God rather than people, and a heated debate ensued. In came Gamaliel – a Pharisee and teacher of the law. He spoke up for the early church, citing a couple of other rebellions that had come to nothing. 'I advise you,' he told his colleagues, 'let them go, for if their purpose or activity is of human origin it will fail, but if it is from God you will not be able to stop these men, you will only find yourself fighting against God.'

As Gamaliel said, I'm sure that if these ideas we dream up aren't from God, then nothing will come of them. If that's not a good reason to get up off our butts, I don't know what is.

A few years ago a group of us decided to start up some kind of church that took cues from the world that most people were used to. We set the venue up like a café, with round tables, background tunes and decent things to drink and eat. On each table was a menu, with a relevant Bible passage or newspaper clipping on the reverse. It was all very relaxed, and during the evening we would have time to hang out together, as well as perhaps a time of worship – sometimes with music and sometimes without.

Later, some others of us also started a club night in

nearby Kingston. We pulled in some good DJs like Cameron Dante and hired out a local venue to put on an event we called RAW. While it wasn't strictly what you would call church, it was a good place for people to meet, chat, dance and find themselves worshipping God and enjoy a good night out without the attendant problems associated with a lager-fuelled night out on the town. It was a different and creative form of some of the aspects that church can embrace; we had people worshipping on the dance floor, prophecies being given from the DJ booth. It was fresh and exciting and open to all.

Whether it's innovative church-planting or starting new companies to excel in the marketplace we need to take more risks without the fear of what other people who choose to live safe lives might say if we fail. Machiavelli the Prince was a diplomat in fifteenth-century Italy. He said this:

There is nothing more difficult to carry out nor more doubtful of success, nor more dangerous to handle than to initiate a new order of things. For the reformer has enemies in all who profit by the old order, and only lukewarm defenders in all those who profit from the new order. This lukewarmness arises partly from fear of adversaries, who have law in their favour, and partly from the incredulity of humankind, who do not truly believe in anything new until they have actual experience of it.

It is very clear from these words that any leader who dreams of changing the way things are, anyone who sticks their hand up for a bit of reform – be that social, cultural, political, ethical or spiritual – will meet opposition. Conflict, isolation and loneliness are all on the menu, and the portions are big. By definition the pioneer will meet opposition. Pushing against boundaries and barriers – even if they just happen to be those put in place by our own doubts and insecurities – guarantees the arrival of difficulty. But difficulty doesn't automatically mean failure; it can just as easily be an opportunity for success.

Throughout the growth of Joshua Generation – from nappies to today's primary school phase – there have been plenty of times when I've come up against opposition. Sometimes I've felt like jacking the whole thing in and giving up, but the times when things have gone well have given just enough nourishing encouragement to keep on going.

But how do you keep on going? What if you don't happen to be made of particularly stubborn stuff? The way that I have managed it so far has been, simply, prayer and perseverance. Two of the most outstanding politicians of the twentieth century – Winston Churchill and Margaret Thatcher – knew what it was to face opposition and persevere. Churchill said, 'Success is moving from one failure to another without losing self-esteem' and Thatcher said, 'You may have to fight a battle more than once to win.' I can remember times when there was absolutely no money in the bank, and, having prayed, I thought it would be right to list twenty people who I knew and call them up and ask for money. There have been other times too when expanding the project has been hard work, only made possible by wearing out both my knees and the phone. But that's what it takes.

'I bet you wish you'd taken the blue pill' is the classic line from *The Matrix*. The truth is that Neo doesn't wish he had taken the blue pill – yes, reality hurts, but it is infinitely preferable to the illusion in which he spent the majority of his life. Having taken the red pill he finally perceives the truth about life. We need leaders like that today; ones who are up for a rough ride, so long as it's the right ride.

Too many of us get weighed down by the pressure on us to be transactional people – the sort who accept the system, withdraw our life-blood from the ATM and shop in the supermarket on Thursday at 6.57 p.m. We can live our life as a transaction, accepting our lot much as we accept whatever is on the menu at McDonald's. Or we can opt for being transformational leaders – ones who are determined to bring out more of the God flavours in the world. Those destiny seekers who are discontent with the way things are will break out of the constraining systems and give themselves to transforming the world in which we live to make it better.

The Truman Show captures a similar concept of the choice between harsh reality and cushy illusion. Having decided to opt for the former, Truman faces Christof – his 'creator':

Christof: Listen to me, Truman. You can leave if you want, I won't try to stop you. But you won't survive out there. You don't know what to do, where to go.

Truman: I have a map.

Christof: Truman, I've watched you your whole life, I saw you taking your first step, your first word, your first kiss. I know you better than you know yourself. You are not going to walk out that door.

Truman: You never had a camera inside my head.

Truman's courageous decision to break out of the small world, to shrug off the constraints that held him back indicates an attitude worth adopting ourselves.

Whatever your dreams – and I hope that you're in the habit of listening to yours and taking them seriously – the basic principles for getting them transferred to reality are the same. Be open, imaginative, communicative, committed, creative, confident and humble. You'll meet more trouble than you thought but keep pushing on and praying, and the result will come. Destiny. It takes work.

Action

1 What is your lifelong dream? If you have never tried conceptualising it, try writing it down, drawing it, or recording it on a Dictaphone.

2 What are some of the obstacles you have faced in your work? How have you got past them?

3 If you are leading in your workplace or church you

will probably be facing opposition now. Take time out to identify the opposition you are facing and then take space to pray your way through it.

5

The Empowerer

It wasn't that long ago that I had a head-on collision with one of the most fundamental of fundamental truths. I had spent the previous twenty-two years pootling along in a state of blissful unawareness, but within minutes of standing up to preach at St Jude's, Little Chalfont, everything had changed. I discovered that many people would rather float serenely on a glassy-calm lake than have their boat rocked by some wild truth.

Admittedly I saw it coming, and I knew I would be likely to get some kind of reaction – but an exodus? I had been asked to preach on 'Reaching Youngsters with the Good News'. Youngsters, I had thought when I opened the invitation letter some months before, was not a good sign. The term belonged alongside Beat Groups, Hit Parade and Golly Gosh. Still, I had got on well with the vicar when we had met the previous summer, and I knew that he was keen to try and bring his polite yet sedated congregation slightly more up to date with the times.

Because of this I thought it was an ideal opportunity for my Empowerer talk. After the reading and a couple of hymns I approached the lectern, drank nervously from my glass of water and held on.

'I believe that God is into sex, money, drugs and power.'

There wasn't exactly silence as I finished my opening move; you could hear selected frantic rustlings as a dedicated few turned to their Bibles to return fire with chapter and verse, while the others coughed threateningly.

I turned and delivered the follow-up that usually brings a sigh of relief. At St Jude's it only made things worse. I explained how I believed that sex was a wonderful gift from God to be used within a lifelong relationship between a man and a woman in marriage, but that it also could be abused in an increasing number of perverse and immoral ways.

More Bible rustling.

I went on to say that I thought there was nothing at all wrong with money – it is good and holy, and any that we do have we usually work darn hard for and we deserve every pound. Sadly, though, it can also be abused, lusted after and focused on to the exclusion of all the other good things God has placed in the world.

More coughing.

Drugs and alcohol: Jesus turned water into wine and Paul told Timothy that 'a little wine' was good for the health. On the other hand it can be abused and end up as the destructive force that brings down relationships and ruins lives. As for drugs, let's be honest and admit that we all use them; whether they are prescribed for medicinal purposes or legal for relaxation and recreation. Of course, they too can wreak havoc.

Aggressive coughing now accompanied by gasps and audible whispers of 'the rascal's off his head'.

As for power, well isn't it true that God manages to have all the power in the world at the same time as remaining good and pure? Like all these other things, power is not inherently bad, but it can be mistreated. It can be the tool of oppression and the supporter of injustice, but it can also be the breaker of oppression as well as the deliverer of justice.

With my introduction complete, I looked up to see a number of backs turned as a portion of the congregation left. It was a shame, especially as I don't think the content was that radical.

I had some more thoughts on this when I was reading Richard Branson's autobiography *Losing My Virginity*. Until I got to the relevant bits, I had never realised how close Branson was to fellow-entrepreneur Freddy Laker. Reading the text it became clear that through their relationship Laker had been able pass on valuable knowledge and wisdom gained from his own experiences fighting British Airways in the early 1980s. It seems as though there is a chance that Branson will now be helping Laker get back into the game, returning the favour. It all made for fascinating reading, especially as it made me think a good deal about empowerment. There is also the perspective that BA abused the virtual monopoly they have in the market to crush any sort of competition.

I started to play a game of mental join-the-dots, making a connection between Branson's empowerment and Disney's *The Lion King*. The scene where the young cub Simba is given to one of the other creatures of his father's kingdom for the purpose of being nurtured and educated had me all excited; here again was another example of the importance of passing on knowledge and experience, a process we call mentoring.

The word 'mentor' is actually derived from a story of a king who was about to lead his army in battle. Unsure of his chances of returning alive, he entrusted the care and education of his young son to a man at court. His job would be to teach the boy to be a king, to lead, fight and grow in wisdom. The man's name was Mentor.

Culturally, mentoring is an integral part of the advancement of any society. Think about Merlin and Arthur, Yoda and Luke Skywalker, Don Quixote and Sancho Panza. The Bible is no stranger to the theme either, with such notables featuring as: Abraham and Isaac, Jacob, Moses and Joshua, Elijah and Elisha, Paul and Timothy, Paul and Titus, Jesus and all the disciples, but especially Peter, James and John. From beginning to end the book is full of these one-on-one mentoring and empowering relationships.

Clive Calver always tells this story when he talks about mentoring. In his early years, South American evangelist Luis Palau had invited Clive to travel with him for a few weeks. Occasionally, in the middle of his talks he would stop and tell the audience that Clive would take it from there on in. Clive says that he has never listened to another preacher so intently as he did whenever Luis was at the mike – as the call to take over could come at any time. He took Clive into press conferences and introduced him to loads of people. While he was only carrying Luis' bags, Clive learnt so much during the time they spent together as he empowered him. The story has always struck me as being a fine example of one great man drawing the greatness out of another, who in turn has done the same to many others.

24/7 Assimilation

The Salvation Army in New South Wales, Australia has a worker, Brenton, who they employ as a mentor to their youth ministries. Brenton's job is to spend quality time each month with the leaders of their fourteen youth works in that region. He sees his role as a coach to these youth leaders. He encourages them in their walk with God and integrity in relationships, and empowers them to set aims and goals for their work.

In my mind, mentoring gets summed up in the Law

of Unconscious Assimilation. This states that we actually become like those people with whom we spend the most frequent and meaningful time – whether we like it or not. In that way mentoring should be encouraged as spending time with someone that you aspire to be like, someone whose gifts, character and strengths you would like to rub off on yourself.

This rubbing off of character to each other is basically what happened with Moses when he spent time with God up the mountain as recorded in Exodus 34. People were amazed to see him when he descended as he literally shone with the glory of God, and his face was so radiant that he needed to wear a veil. When we spend time with God, the same thing can happen to us. We don't have to be always fanatically reading the Bible or singing and prophesying round the clock. Instead just sitting there in his presence and company can be enough to let some of his character rub off onto us.

Richard Foster wrote in *Celebration of Discipline* that: 'God has given us the disciplines of the spiritual life as a means of receiving grace. The disciplines allow us to place ourselves before God so he can transform us.' When we find places that we can be with God and experience his presence, just to sit there with God for some time actually introduces the possibility that we might be transformed, which is a tremendous thing to be aiming for.

I remember that on a trip to LA a friend and I made sure that we went to Hollywood Boulevard. Alongside the imprints of movie stars and celebrities from time past, we headed straight for one plaque in particular – Billy Graham's. We both aspire to be really good preachers and having our photo taken next to Bill's square made for a nice memory. Walking away from it, we both talked excitedly about how great it would be to be able to communicate with some of the effectiveness of a man like Graham. It was certainly something to dream about.

This is precisely the principle of mentoring: finding someone that you aspire to be like in some way and hanging out with them in the hope that something of their character and gifts may rub off on you. Aspiration is an essentially natural and instinctive emotion, and we have managed to build a whole celebrity cult around it. Just think, if we didn't want to be like them, why on earth would we spend our early teenage years following some bambi-eyed popster from far away? That doesn't mean we should sack the whole idea though, as following someone who is following God can offer numerous rewards. Paul knew the score on this point and told Timothy to imitate him as he imitated Christ.

So, with mentoring relationships established as a thoroughly good thing, you may be wondering how you can start doing it. Whether you're up for being a mentee, looking for someone to mentor you, or you're up for encouraging someone yourself, it can be important to follow a few basic steps along the way.

The first step is getting a heart for mentoring, getting into the whole idea of people being influenced and empowered, being helped to excel at the things God has placed within. It means being receptive to or having yourself a sense of aspiration in relation to another person's relationship with God.

Second, it is vital that you intentionally identify someone who you would like to mentor or be mentored by. They may need to have similar giftings or a similar vocation so that the whole process will have a sense of cohesion and common purpose.

Third, you will need to initiate the relationship. It's like going out with someone: you get to know the person first of all, go out a few times and see if you are compatible. That way you don't get into something quickly which you very soon regret. Then you can verbalise what you are looking for in the relationship and communicate your intent.

Once that is established it is necessary to talk openly about the mentoring process that will take place between you. What exactly are your expectations? What are the practical details, such as when, where and how often will you meet?

Fifth, it's time just to get on and do the business. It's up to you both to make it work, and that means there can be no substitute for action.

Finally, it is absolutely vital that you regularly evaluate the process, particularly from the view of the person being mentored. If it isn't helping them to discover their potential in God, then it could be time to call it a day. There's nothing worse than dragging it out if it really is not working, so honesty is vital. Having said that, a good bit of hard graft can bring things around, so make sure that you're as honest as possible in your communication at this stage.

With this set-up phase sorted, it can be confusing trying to work out exactly how the mentoring process should move forward. There are seven things that I look for during a mentoring relationship.

Relationship

At the end of the day mentoring is about a relationship. Mentoring is not a programme, nor is it a systematic process that refuses to budge if you try to shift it. It is about two people working together, giving freely of themselves and developing trust. There also needs to be a growing awareness and a knowledge of each other.

Discipleship

Put simply, mentoring is about helping another person be a more effective follower of Jesus Christ. It's about helping someone else chase and pursue God, to discover their destiny and dreams, helping them to walk where God wants them to walk.

Affirmation

Having someone who believes in you may be a first for some people, but in the mentoring relationship it is not an optional extra. In the same way that God spoke loud and clear as Jesus was baptised in the Jordan, we all need to know that some people around us are willing us on, certain that our goal is one worth pursuing. It is this affirmation that can encourage people to chase after some of the more nutty ideas that they may have had.

Impartation

This is the essence of what is passed between two people at a deep level. We are not here talking about mere head knowledge. There will be a passing on of: wisdom or what I call distilled knowledge, the Holy Spirit's anointing for a specific task, the development of particular giftings, the rubbing off of godly character and habits. This is where it is helpful if the mentor is actually operating in the same profession as the mentee because there is something which gets stirred up in two people of a similar calling. As Proverbs says, iron sharpens iron.

Empowerment

This comes down to helping someone reach their God-given potential – not by putting greatness into someone, but by drawing out that which is already there, even to the point where the mentee may exceed the mentor in what they achieve.

Connections

Making introductions that could be beneficial is another integral part of the whole deal. Putting in a good word for someone or passing on a contact can make the difference between mentoring that is successful on paper, and that which has worked in practice. Also important is the ability to connect a mentor with resources, books and materials that may be strategic for their development.

Partnership

The relationship that exists between the two is at the heart of it all. Remember, there is strength in unity, but it also can be found in diversity. It needs to allow the mentee to do things differently, to be true to their culture and age without fearing the imposition of the mentor's personal routines. Mentoring is not about cloning, but about encouraging true freedom and individuality from a perspective of humble experience.

In my own life I don't have to look very far to find my own collection of people who have been significant in my growth as an individual. When I first became a Christian at the age of nineteen – having been in church for years – a guy called Arthur met with me every week to pray, talk and study the Bible. I don't think I would ever have been able to pray out loud had it not been for his persistence. I now look at him and his wife Rosemary as my spiritual parents. There are lots of other people who have taken on the role of mentor at different points in my life, and all of them have affected me significantly.

All of this brings me back to St Jude's. You see, I've come to think of God as being the absolute King of mentoring, the last word in empowerment. He is fully in the business of improvements, and with him on our side, the possibilities are enormous. Thinking about sex, money, drugs and power, I am convinced that there is room for God to allow us to discover the full extent of their good possibilities. They may be potentially thorny issues, but is that any reason for us to get uptight and cough defensively whenever they approach? No – God is God, omnipotent and ultimate Creator. He can see the possibilities for the good things that he has created, and is surely keen for us to get on with using them.

Quite simply, Jesus is the ultimate empowerer. Nobody does it better, and you only have to check out the Gospels to back this up. He took twelve men who were full of weakness, failings and personality defects, and managed to disciple and empower them. As he prepared them for his final departure, one of the things that he said to them was this: 'I tell you the truth: anyone who has faith in me will do what I have been doing. He will do even greater things than these because I am going to the father.' This ability to honestly say that he believed his mentees would achieve greater things than he had managed to do is the mark of a truly awesome empowerer.

Today Jesus is with the Father, leaving us with the Holy Spirit, the other 'counsellor – the spirit of truth' that will be with us permanently. The NIV uses the word 'counsellor', while the Authorised Version calls him the 'advocate', the Good News opts for 'helper', but at the end of the day the Holy Spirit is living proof that God is by nature an 'alongside-God', who is not content to remain aloof and distant, but who is desperate to become involved in the minutiae of our lives, for our betterment and his glory. This empowering presence of his is here to help us do the impossible, to carry out that which we would never be able to do were it not for God.

This applies equally well to ourselves. It is unbiblical and foolish to reject the possibilities that lie within each one of us. So what if someone may be slightly wayward; why should we give up on those who only feel comfortable on the fringes of church culture? If we really do believe that God is who he said he is, then we will be ready to draw out the good from the most extreme sources.

Isn't this what Jesus did with the disciples? They were an odd bunch, certainly not Grade A leadership material. Hot-tempered, ignorant and stubborn, they provide the New Testament with some classic humour. Yet in three years Jesus chose them all individually, and empowered them to lead the new God-empowered people movement which became known as Christianity.

One summer on a trip to Turkey, some friends and I visited the ancient city of Ephesus. In the middle of some sightseeing and learning more about the achievements of the Romans, I started to think about what Paul had written to the church in the city. In Ephesians where Paul lists different leadership gifts which people may be given, he goes on to explain that these are given so that leaders can prepare God's people for works of service. It seems to me that so many of us would be happiest being one of the apostles, prophets, evangelists, pastors or teachers in order to do the works of service. It misses the point. Paul doesn't say that these gifts are given so that the leaders can do the works of service but so that the leaders might empower other people to do the works of service.

I've been trying hard to do this sort of thing through Joshua Generation. Instead of arrogantly proclaiming that I am prepared to bestow greatness on humble subjects, dishing it out like the New Year's Honours, I've been working on the assumption that God has already invested much that is great within each one of us. The job that we ought to get on with is working out how best to draw gifts and abilities out of the individuals to help them reach their potential.

There's a young guy called Matt who works with me all the time. When we go to do various seminars and day conferences Matt often leads the worship and I speak. This means that he has the dubious privilege of hearing my talks a number of times over. Lucky guy. Once we were leading a session of seminars where I was going though a series of talks on life-maturing experiences. About six months later Matt was flying off somewhere hot to be the assistant leader on a Christian holiday, something that he had never done before. On the third day tragedy struck and the main leader died. Matt was left to pastor the group through the trauma as well as to carry on with what remained of the holiday. He told me later that he remembered what he had heard me speak about all those months before, and that he managed to get down to business by telling himself that this was about the best example he was ever going to get of one of those life-maturing experiences. He dealt with the whole situation brilliantly and returned home exhausted but with the affirmation that he had faced the situation well.

If it wasn't for Barnabas we probably wouldn't have fourteen of the books that are found in the New Testament. He was a great encourager, and had his finest hour when Saul decided to give up torturing Christians and opted to join them instead. None of the other disciples would believe that it was a genuine transformation, but Barnabas stuck up for the newly named Paul, putting himself on the line until the rest of the crew believed him. Paul went on to write thirteen books in the New Testament and laid many foundations for the church as we know it. So what about the fourteenth book?

Barnabas also encouraged and empowered Mark, standing by him when Paul refused to take him on a particular mission trip because he had let them down on the last team he was a part of. Barnabas continued to see the best in Mark, and was up for giving him another chance. After this sharp dispute Paul chose Silas and left, and Barnabas took Mark and sailed for Cyprus. Mark subsequently produced his own Gospel, which surely would never have happened had not Barnabas picked him up and encouraged him to stick with things throughout his darkest hour.

Through these biblical and personal stories it becomes clear that there is a pattern for the use of power as God intended; it is there for his glory, not for our avoidance. 'Use the force,' Yoda told Luke, and use it we must. What Jesus wanted more than anything was to empower the disciples and see them do even greater things than he had managed to do himself.

But power can be abused, as it was at the Nine O'clock Service in Sheffield. The leader was a highly gifted individual who you could say was abused by power himself, and also became an abuser of power. His clear abilities and the NOS which emerged very quickly under his leadership led him on a fast track to ordination. He was given a lot of responsibility and it seems to me inadequate care and oversight, particularly as NOS moved out of the care of the planting church to a different geographical area, and out of its theological heritage in evangelicalism towards creation theology. It sounds trite but it is true that responsibility without accountability is a liability. Then the leader in turn became an abuser of power both sexually and mentally. The way that power is handled and empowerment takes place is indeed critical.

Tom Peters – one of the gurus of management theory – writes in his book *The Pursuit of Wow*:

Hierarchies are going, going, gone. The average Mary or Mike is being asked to take on extraordinary responsibility. He or she may be on the payroll or, at least as likely, an independent contractor. In any event, the hyper-fast moving, wired up, re-engineered, quality-obsessed organisation – virtual or not – will succeed or fail on the strength of the trust that the remaining, tiny cadre of managers places in the folks working on the front line.

Delegation is certainly on its way out. Instead of superiors handing tasks down to subordinates, we are working on a much more level playing field. Empowerment is about leaders helping others to develop and excel at using their abilities and talents. It has nothing to do with the position that we might enjoy but everything to do with the positive influence we can have on others. There are many individuals whose influence is disproportionate to their status, just as there are many companies or churches whose influence is disproportionate to their size.

There are specific examples in mind. Phil Wall has increasing influence within the Salvation Army as he works for renewal, yet he is not one of the boys in the hierarchy. Then there are people like Rob Frost and John Hibberts working for reformation in the Methodist Church. Again their influence is far greater than the position they have as they serve God and the church. The Pioneer network of about eighty churches and dozens of ministries under the care of Gerald Coates is comparatively small when you begin to think about the huge impact that movement has nationally and internationally.

This is the essence of what it is to be empowered by God; it's about positive influence, not status. It is also another example of the way that Jesus's message turns the established order of things upside down, having influence for the good of others.

At times I feel that we might be living in the middle of a power struggle within the UK. It is not unusual or surprising, as it takes place with every emerging generation. As you look at the different generations it becomes clear that the younger one exits adolescence and adopts a militant and radical desire to change the fabric of society. They do not blindly accept that things will be the way their parents' generation created them, and are by their very nature highly motivated to bring about change.

This power struggle can be pictured as existing between two generations: one is convinced that if only the wrinkled dinosaurs would step back and allow them a chance that things would be much improved. Their attitude often comes across as arrogant and self-righteous, while the second generation adopts a different stance. Being established in the faith and having proved it by their many years, they often see a new generation emerging with some talent, and their insecurity-fired reaction can be to rely on a tightly controlling style of leadership. No surprises then that these people often struggle to empower those emerging.

What we need to see between these two generations is quite simple: we need to have the hearts of the older leaders turn towards the hearts of the younger leaders and vice versa. There needs to be unity and synergy as one generation empowers another to get on with the business of succeeding.

This isn't just confined to church committees and living-room discussions, but is an issue that is very much relevant to the Christian scene. As a new generation of leaders emerges, it makes for interesting viewing to sit back and see how smooth the process is, or isn't in some cases. We need to see the younger leaders turn to their elders and honour them for all they have achieved and will continue to achieve. The mature leaders need to draw gifts out of the younger leaders, and encourage them to practise within the structures put in place and perhaps to create a few of their own. As my friend John Noble has put it, we need to see reconciliation, affirmation, appreciation and even preferment.

When Richard Branson was asked why he had written his autobiography at forty-eight, he said,

It's because I wanted to record the most exciting years, the years of struggle, so young people might be inspired. I want them to follow their dreams, to believe anything is possible. Most entrepreneurs are so busy struggling that they don't have time to record their efforts until they are too old. And with my rather foolish adventures each year, I thought it time I got it down on paper.

Clearly, there are people who do want to encourage,

equip and empower a new generation of leaders to excel. That's a good thing, especially when you're keen on discovering your destiny.

Action

1 Who are the people who have inputted into your life in significant ways or at significant times? Perhaps write them a card or telephone and say thank you.

2 Who are the people that you aspire to be like in some way? Make sure that you do everything you can to see these people on a regular basis.

3 Who are the people that you think you could helpfully mentor? Ask them out to lunch and begin to develop a relationship with them.

6

The Builder

I hate football. No, that's not quite right. Football and I are going through a trial separation. I used to play with friends at school, but ever since I found out that I was about as useful with the old pig's bladder as a pig without a bladder, I've been sulking and have refused to acknowledge the presence of the game. Slightly immature, I know, but that's the way it is. So there. When the nation gets gripped by World Cup fever and the fair-weather supporters come out of their armchairs and start talking about the game they hardly know, I am forced to find something less boring to occupy my time with, like growing a goatee.

So it was to my intense dismay that I have just sat through 122 minutes of England's finest lousing the whole thing up against some middle-European unpronounceables. I don't know if the common consensus is that we were robbed, but it looked more to me as if we were desperate to give the goals away much as a terrorist might want to rid himself of an un-pinned grenade. As if that wasn't bad enough, there were at least sixteen minutes of clichés and shiny suits from the studio at half-time. I think I feel a bit faint.

This all started earlier when a group who are on a Joshua Generation training course were coming round to my flat for a social. I was just about to make the necessary preparations for an evening BBQ and some silly games when one of them called me up to tell me that they all wanted to watch the football. Not wanting to sound like an idiot I muttered a weary 'of course' and went out to buy a TV aerial. Just what I needed, I thought, a slow death at the hands of Saint and Greavsie. I felt ill.

After the people had arrived and settled down to the match, I was kind of surprised when I looked at my watch and saw that I had been watching – without any serious physical side effects – for almost an hour. Not that I was enjoying it, you understand, but some things were going on during the match that caught my eye. I decided to sit it out to the end, working out what it was that was holding my attention.

Now my guests have gone I can put my thoughts down on paper. I'm sure I'm not going to get offered any work as a commentator on the strength of these thoughts, but they made sense to me at the time. Here goes:

There was more than one player on the pitch. That means that somehow, through teamwork, the players were united with their colleagues. They knew where they should be, and expected the rest to play according to an established plan.

They all had different roles. Mr Goalie obviously had it easy as he didn't have to do any running, and he got to wear gloves. The ones at the front got to take the glory while the others further back had to stop the other team's glory boys from reaching Mr Goalie. They all behaved slightly differently, and in the case of the Bulgarians, it paid off.

My third observation was that each man on the pitch was continually active. OK, they may have stopped to try and impress the crowd with some fairly poor acting and injury-feigning but, apart from that, the pitch was a throbbing mass of energy from start to finish.

Finally I noticed that they all had the same aim – even the opposite teams were united in that. It was essentially simple (although it wasn't for England): it was all about goals. Balls in the back of the net was what it came down to and the boys did us proud.

If Paul was writing his letters to Corinth, Ephesus and the Romans today I don't think he'd be using the picture of a body (unless his audience were a bunch of medics or body-piercers). He would use the illustration of a football team, because as I realised (under sufferance), each member has a different role to play in order to secure a victory for the whole team. Without one member of the team, the whole unit would be dysfunctional; a fact which Paul was well aware of himself. *The Message* puts it like this:

> You can easily see how this kind of thing works by looking no further than your own body. Your body has many parts – limbs, organs, cells – but no matter how many parts you can name, you're still one body . . . I want you to think about how all this makes you more significant, not less. A body isn't just a single part blown up into something huge. It's all the different-but-similar parts arranged and functioning together . . . The way God designed our bodies is a model for understanding our lives together as a church: every part dependent on every other part, the parts we mention and the parts we don't, the parts we see and the parts we don't. (1 Corinthians 12)

We have lived through an era of individualism over the last few years that will shape our nation for generations to come. Cast your mind back to the philosophy of Descartes – he of 'I think therefore I am' fame. His tract can be applied to a whole series of clones: materialism (I own therefore I am), consumerism (I shop therefore I am), existentialism (I feel therefore I am).

Politics then followed this mindset to its logical conclusion. In an interview with *Woman's Own* magazine, Margaret Thatcher said, 'There is no such thing as society.

There are individual men and women, and their families.' Capitalism has focused our attention solely on ourselves: our money, our lives, our choices and our hopes. A strong sense of the collective and community went out of the window with pounds, shillings and pence.

If you think about philosophy and politics, and particularly the influence of evangelical theology throughout this century, there can be no greater standard-bearer than Billy Graham. His campaigns throughout the world sent out a call to individuals to return to Jesus. We too have encouraged this, placing a lot of emphasis on the individual's relationship with God rather than on developing a sense of community or mutual belonging between groups of Christians. But it hasn't just been politics and theology that have leant towards individualism.

Back to Basics

Contrasting with this emphasis on individualism, the New Testament preaches a message of mutual responsibility. Out of twenty-one letters that appear in the second half of the Bible, only three are addressed to individuals. As we read through the New Testament we come across the phrase 'one another' again and again, as the writers deliver their manifesto of love, acceptance, support, community, devotion and mutual respect.

The leader who is a builder stands apart from individualism and stands with a team. The builder is someone who works to nurture individuals into a highly committed and motivated team working towards a common purpose.

The Gallup Organisation's book *First, Break All The Rules* records research taken in 24 companies in 2,500 business units collecting information from 105,000 employees. It identifies twelve questions which are linked to any company's productivity, profitability, retention of employees and customer satisfaction. These questions show the importance of the builder in creating a sense of team and a decent working environment.

1 Do I know what is expected of me at work?
2 Do I have the materials and equipment I need to do my work right?
3 At work, do I have the opportunity to do what I do best every day?
4 In the last seven days, have I received recognition or praise for good work?
5 Does my supervisor or someone at work seem to care about me as a person?
6 Is there someone at work who encourages my development?
7 At work, do my opinions seem to count?
8 Does the mission/purpose of my company make me feel like my work is important?
9 Are my co-workers committed to doing quality work?
10 Do I have a best friend at work?

11 In the last six months, have I talked with someone about my progress?

12 At work, have I had opportunities to learn and grow?

The questions are the simplest and most accurate method of assessing the strength of any workplace environment, team or team builder. A team builder needs to be able to know, value, motivate, care, and develop their team, providing opportunities to stretch them.

As I've said earlier, I like going to the theatre. There's nothing like a bit of culture to get me going, and I love trying to interpret the meanings behind the performance with friends on the journey home. One play that stuck in my mind was a production of J. B. Priestley's *An Inspector Calls*. Funnily enough the plot goes something like this: an inspector calls at a house after a suspected murder has taken place. He calls a halt to the dinner party and demands that no one should leave. The next couple of hours are spent with him doing some thorough detective work, enough eventually to name the killer. But instead of it being Mr Plum in the study with the candlestick, it turns out that the inspector reveals to each person how they are partly responsible for the suicide of Eva Smith. Either they made her life difficult, lost her a job, dumped her or whatever else.

Sadly, at the end of the play there are only two characters left on the stage – the others have returned to their dinner party upstairs – indicating that they are the only ones to have accepted the parts that they played in the young woman's death.

Coming home on the train, my head was being pounded by the message: am I my brother's keeper? Am I responsible for those people that I meet and live around? Want to know the answer? It is a resounding 'yes'. I believe that we all need to try hard to understand more fully what it means to live as a community, to have a decent sense of commitment to and responsibility for those around us. We need to think in terms of groups rather than individuals, us instead of me. Why? Well, if we are to discover our destiny and move off into the bright and easy sunset (yeah, right), we need to learn the vital lesson of the builder: none of us on our own has all the gifts that we need. Instead we will need to find and lean on other members who can help carry the torch. Teamwork is about wholeness, as well as success.

There is an interesting development in the corporate sector at present which is a counter to individualism and is known as 'corporate responsibility'. SP (short for Simon-Piers), a friend from my church, has recently relocated with his wife to Budapest, Hungary, where he is establishing a European marketing agency consulting with companies to help them take seriously their responsibility to society and the world. This agency, already well established in the UK, is designing projects which help refocus oil companies to reinvest in the Earth, and supermarket chains like Tesco invest in computers for schools. This is another indicator that we are about to see a greater shift from individualism to a community focus.

Ponchos Get Everywhere

I often think of this when I see buskers on the street. There used to be a rather bizarre creature knocking about the place known as a one-man-band. They looked pretty stupid and their music was a poor relation of German oompah music – you know, the sort you listen to when you're wearing those little leather shorts and drinking beer. I haven't seen one in years, and I'm convinced that they've all taken up employment as telesales agents – such is their complete obliviousness to public opinion. In their place have come the poncho-wearing pan-pipe bands from South America. Actually, I think it's just one extraordinarily well-travelled band as I'm sure I've seen the same one in at least five different European cities. You can find them for yourself; just head for the main square of any capital city and they'll be there, jigging about as they play their pipes, guitars and drums. It's always a great experience, not least because they seem like such a tight unit. I'd have difficulty recognising any individuals, but shove them together and I'd spot them a mile off.

This change in street-commerce/entertainment mirrors an equally radical change that has taken place of late within the church itself. It wasn't long ago that churches were led by pastors who epitomised the spirit of the one-man-band. Give them half a chance and they'd not only be preaching, leading the worship and doing the readings, but opening and locking up, counting the money and leading the playgroup for young mothers. It was madness and it was very common.

Slowly things began to change, and today we find ourselves – although still in a definite period of transition – living in a radically different climate from that of previous years. Now we are settling down with the spirit of teamwork. Pastors and vicars gather around them individuals to whom are entrusted sizable chunks of the church's life – whether that be youth work, worship, pastoring or administration. I like this, and I am convinced that it is making for a stronger church with much increased longevity and greater opportunity to embrace other individuals, as well as increasing the life-expectancy of the pastor. The days of the Lone Ranger Christian are dead. Long live the ponchos.

When I was in my early twenties I attended theological college with a view to being ordained. 'Theological college' is the wrong term, and I feel convinced that the place is much better summed up as an 'institutional clerical processing and canning plant'. But Matt, you may gasp, why the cynicism? The answer is pretty simple really, as at the time I felt that instead of allowing me to become who I was supposed to be, I was being wedged by the course into a very tight mould of what the establishment (those who enjoy being in charge and letting others know it) thought a vicar should be. It wasn't fun.

We all arrived at the start of the course, prepared to discover the hidden life with God. Unfortunately the curriculum was fixed and didn't allow much space for surprises or spontaneous divine interruptions – something I've always thought was a shame. Individuality and uniqueness were cleared away from the table, and a stodgy helping of 'grade A vicar' was served in their place.

By contrast I have many great memories of the time that I have spent with a particular leader called Rob. He has always seen areas that my gifts can be used in, and while the roles and tasks I have been given have often stretched me further than I thought possible, I've always been very highly motivated. The roles and tasks that I have been given have struck me as ripe ground for my talents, and I am convinced that the experiences as part of his team have helped shape and mature me. I was empowered.

I believe that each of us is unique and special. Being part of a team is to discover some of those mysteries that lie within each of us. Teamwork isn't about conformity, but interdependence: realising that there are others who can do things that you can't do (and vice versa), and that together you can get a good deal more accomplished.

Interestingly, the market research company, the Gallup Organisation, has spent quite a lot of time researching training and personnel development. It would seem that the vast majority of companies spend a large amount of their resources trying to get employees to be better at things they are not good at. This makes no sense to people like those at Gallup (as well as to just about every other management consultant worth their salt). Instead, they suggest that training budgets be redirected towards enabling people to excel at things they are already good at. I think this is a vitally important lesson waiting to go up on the church's blackboard. Not only has God created us with gifts – knitting us together in our mothers' wombs with specific talents and abilities – but he has recreated us when we are born again. At this point he invests in us new gifts and talents through the power of his Holy Spirit. And so we need to learn how to identify what our individual gifts and abilities are, assessing how they all can fit into a team context.

Gallup writes about perceiving talent:

Understanding the role of talent in a corporate culture allows an organisation to pinpoint and fulfil human resource needs better than ever before. Over the past quarter of a century of studying success in a variety of fields, Gallup has developed employee selection instruments that ensure that the right person is hired for the right job. These programs demonstrate why there are no bad employees, just poor match-ups between an individual's skills and talents and the requirements of the job.

According to Gallup, God and a few other enlight-ened ones, every individual is gifted and able. There are no worthless or talentless workers, just poor match-ups between task and individual.

Jesus told a story about talents – although they weren't the sort that we're thinking of. Instead he was telling people about a master who was going away for some time, and who decided to give certain sums of money to three of his servants. To one he gave five, to another he gave two and to the third he gave one. He left them to use their newly acquired resources as they saw fit. Upon his return he found the five-talent man to be waving a bag with ten talents, and the two-talent man to have four in his mitts. Both had invested and made a good return, receiving the praise of their master for their trouble. The sad bloke who had one hadn't bothered to work it, choosing instead to bury it in the ground for safe keeping. The master was not best pleased with him, and decided to get rid of him.

Should this story remind us of anyone? Perhaps God is the master and our personal talents ought to be honed, flexed and improved throughout the duration of our own separation from the master. Perhaps we should be looking for ways to use them, to get them working in the kingdom and see some fruit, rather than sit on them and take it easy.

As Timothy was told by his mentor, Paul, discovering the life he was created to live needed to be fuelled by actions that would 'fan into flame the gift of God' that he had received when the elders had laid their hands on him. Paul went on to encourage him not to neglect his gifts, and we too need to adopt the message as our own.

Leaving talents to lie dormant and fossil-like within is, quite frankly, a waste. Like any muscle, the more we use our gifts the stronger they become, and the less the risk of them atrophying.

Not surprisingly I went through my fair share of struggles when I became a Christian. You name it, I went through it: guilt, confusion, apathy and temptation. There was one particular instance that stands out above the rest, and it happened when I was part of a team. Every other member was incredibly gifted; they all played musical instruments like angels and managed to hold a serene smile for anything up to twenty-three and a half hours each day. They were all at least grade eight in their respective instruments, while I was only just about able to tell you which end of a violin you shouldn't tread on. I felt terrible about the whole thing and was convinced that I had nothing to give.

Thankfully, at some point all this despair transmuted itself into a sense of rigorous frustration that I too wasn't in the running for the title of Young Musician of the Year. At a particular event I attended I made up my mind to take Paul up on the advice he gave the Corinthians and 'eagerly desire gifts'. I sat down and wrote out a list of gifts that I wanted to develop. Looking back on it now I'm prepared to admit that the ability to prophesy to nations, raise the dead and float six feet above ground may have been a tad ambitious, but I know for sure that it gave me something to focus on. I soon realised that the floating wasn't on the menu, but the others (including leadership, visionary, evangelism and generally being a good friend) were all up for grabs. I put in the hours both in prayer and in research, reading up about them and compiling a mental dossier of what it took to grow in such ways as a Christian.

You see, the desire to work together must be complemented by a desire to better oneself. The kind of destiny that lies at the end of serious and slack easing back into the couch of personal apathy is not worth an awful lot. Instead we all need a double portion of zeal for personal development. Forgive me if I sound like a fanatical self-helper here, but there is no way around it; we simply have to expand on our skills. It's biblical, practical and after all, intensely satisfying.

Teamwork

There were three men who were regular hunters in the wilds of Northern America. Turning up to their log cabin one night, they prepared themselves for bed and drank whatever whiskey, ate whatever beans and chewed whatever tobacco they needed to before they went to sleep. The next morning Chad and Butch (for sake of argument, you understand) awoke to find their pal, Siegfried, missing. They searched throughout the cabin, and had just got around to not worrying and considering the preparation of their breakfast when they heard a frantic scream come from outside. Quickly they opened the door and were confronted by the sight of their friend running through the woods towards them, screaming, being followed by a rather animated-looking bear. Siegfried was only feet away from the grizzly, but Chad and Butch reckoned that they would have just enough time to close the door behind the unlucky jogger and so save him from the bear. Guessing that this was their plan, Siegfried continued to sprint towards the door, but at the last minute he changed direction. He sidestepped the door and crashed into the wall. The bear did not follow him, but remained on course. Chad and Butch slammed the door shut. Just as they realised what had happened, Siegfried − ever the jester − peered in at the window and shouted, 'You sort that one out, I'll be back with another in five minutes.' My, how they laughed.

This fine example of teamwork illustrates the difference between two common extremes of personality types. One may favour the thrill of immediate action, making things happen and delivering the goods, while another may operate on a slower, more long-term basis. In extreme cases these types can represent the differences between evangelists and pastors. The evangelist may be happy just to grab the new convert or disciple while the pastor will be more concerned with the long-term issues surrounding their growth and nurture. The truth is that each team needs people that complement each other through their diversity, rather than muddling each other with their similarity. There can be nothing quite so exciting as seeing a group of people working together and sharpening each other's strengths and abilities, whether this be in a church or in a school, hospital or business. It is the excitement of knowing that a future is about to be shaped.

Personally I build team in a number of ways. First, by understanding the process of building a team. A team does not come together and automatically operate. There is a process by which a team moves from forming – getting to know each other; to storming – becoming aware of each other's differences and what that means in terms of being able to interrelate; to norming – when people become used to each other and grasp an understanding of how the other team members operate and communicate. And finally there's performing, where a team reaches its peak of performance and operation towards its commonly held goal.

Second, build a team which takes ownership. A team will never take ownership if all the decisions are made for them. A team will take ownership if they share the decision-making process, the setting of deadlines, and the ownership of projects. For example, with Joshua Generation team members I always ask them what projects they would like to manage and ask them to set their own deadlines.

Third, and perhaps one of the most important aspects of team building is the opportunity to develop relationships and have fun. When new team members join Joshua Generation their first day of work is a rest day, if that makes sense. When the first graduate, Matt Stuart, joined Joshua Generation, we went for a day's cycle ride followed by a sauna and a Jacuzzi. The fun element continues. Recently when I was speaking in Stoke-on-Trent one evening we took the day out to go to Alton Towers, threatening to lose our lunch on some ride named Oblivion.

Fourth, building a team is about keeping a focus. It's easy for individuals and teams to end up getting obsessed with things that are not their business. It is the role of the team leader, the builder, to keep that focus sharp, to keep the vision clear in the minds of the team members, making sure that goal is the same for all.

The art of drawing together a diverse group of people, developing their ownership of the common goal, facilitating friendship and fun and enabling each team member to perform to their very best; this is what it means to discover our destiny to be builders.

Action

1 Make a list of the different teams that you are a part of and consider what role you assume in each team.

2 Consider the main team of people that you work with. Pray and thank God for the ways each of them has a different personality and giftings (compared to you).

3 Why not suggest a fun night out for the team that you work with? If you are in the position to, perhaps the company could pay for the meal, quasar or whatever you do.

7

The Relater

Thursday 8.36 p.m.

Studying at college can get so dull, don't you think? This is Sheffield, 1991, and the highlights of the last few weeks have been a departure from the administration faculty and a new brand of liquid soap being introduced to the men's cloakroom on the lower floor. That is why we are all so excited about what happens next.

It was the idea of one of the postgraduate students – one who previously studied at some seminary in middle America where he wasn't allowed to go to the cinema or eat cheese (no, I never understood that one either). Anyway, when they weren't picketing movie theatres or dairy farms, they occasionally got round to having what they called an Angel Week. This involved each person writing their own name on a piece of paper and placing it in a hat. Once all the residents' names were in, the hat was then passed around again and each person took out a bit of paper. For the next week they had to secretly do wonderful things for the person they had picked. That way, everyone got to be both angel and mortal, enjoying the dual thrill of giving and receiving.

The hat man came around an hour ago and collected my own piece of paper. I had thought long and hard about how I wanted to present myself on paper, and eventually opted for the impoverished look; writing on the back of an overdrawn bank statement in blunted pencil. I made sure that my sort code and account number were gently underlined. Genius.

Thursday 8.54 p.m.
Mr Hat has just returned and I made my choice. I picked Becky, one of the nicest people around. Pooh. How do you do something nice for someone who's already so nice? I mean, if they were a socially challenged miser then any old act of charity would seem good, yeah? This is going to be harder than I thought.

Friday 9.13 a.m.
I've just got back from the cash point, where my current account balance is still alarmingly well below zero. Perhaps the angel is a slow starter. Actually I feel better as I've just realised that any credits placed in my account

would take a few days to clear. I thank God for their generosity.

Friday 4.27 p.m.

While packing for a weekend away I notice my severe lack of clean clothes. I can just about make it through the weekend, but Monday will be tough (as well as smelly). A stroke of genius has just touched me, and I hastily prepare a note which I pin to my twin black bags of dirty washing. 'Dear Angel, Please put my whites in on a hot wash. Non biological preferred. Thanks, your Mortal' it says. Pleased with my succinct approach to Angel Week I leave the bags and note outside my room and dash out for the weekend.

Saturday 5.30 p.m.

Having just realised that my absence has put a slight damper on my angelic activities in the interest of Becky, I decide to do what I can given my current circumstances (i.e. 70 miles away and having too good a time to spoil it by thinking about college). I decide to get straight to the point and deliver a stunningly accurate prophecy that will reduce her to tears as well as her knees, encouraging her greatly and enabling her to walk into the glorious freedom that God is offering her. I find a postcard shop and write 'Becky, God loves you. A lot.' The delivery of that nugget having been entrusted to the care of the Royal Mail, I get back to the serious business of catching up with my old friends.

Sunday 6.42 p.m.

I've just got back and I'm not happy. My clothes are
nowhere to be seen – laundered or otherwise. I hope my
angel is working on it all right now or I'm going to have
a boxer-short-free week. Not a good prospect. Add to
that the fact that I don't feel well, and things aren't
looking too good. I decide to get an early night. I'll say
a prayer for Becky just before sleep though, just to give
her a double blessing.

Monday 7.14 a.m.

The first five minutes of the day weren't good. I awoke
in a cold sweat, with my mouth feeling like the wrong
end of an ashtray and my limbs aching as though I had
been back to the gym. Once I had struggled out of bed
and left my room to get a drink, things started to look
up. Not only had the angel visited, but it had deposited
my freshly washed laundry, ironed to perfection with
each item separated by tissue paper and all wrapped up
in a huge bow. What an angel.

Friday

The rest of the week has been a rollercoaster of goodness
and warm sympathy. While I have been tucked up in my
bed, my doorstep has become the secret dropping-off
point for a range of treats that have made my life worth
living: from pills to magazines, fruit to missed seminar
notes (OK, not so sure about that one, but it's the thought
that counts). Hope Becky was pleased with her card. I'm

thinking about suggesting that we play Angel Week once a month as it would solve all my washing problems.

I'll Be There For You

Our lives are spent surrounded by a complex web of relationships. They form the network through which pass such ingredients as work, home, church and friends. Wherever we go – whatever we do – we cannot avoid the fact that we are influencing other people. Having thought about this, I've come to the conclusion that this generation can be described as a friends generation; generally, we fifteen- to thirty-year-olds and others of a similar life perspective place a good deal of importance on both friendships and relationships. We have very little sense of commitment towards institutions and organisations, and choose instead to direct our primary focus towards those whom we see as being part of our own interpersonal network.

Living in London has some huge advantages, and I'm continually amazed at the amount of undiscovered cultural treats there are waiting to be discovered. Taking a wider look, I also enjoy seeing how the trends in the city both prompt and mirror larger trends happening within culture at large. Over the last few years one such development has been the emergence of the café culture. Take a trip into town on a summer's evening and you feel as though you're on the continent; outside dining is an option, and people sit, eat, drink and watch the world go by, enjoying and helping to create a wonderfully relaxed atmosphere.

This café culture pivots on the interaction of friends. As I'm writing this I'm obviously thinking about the TV series, and I'm sure that as well as the gags, part of the reason for the success of the show is the fact that many in our culture would dearly love to emulate their lifestyle. I'm not just talking about the fact that they're all beautiful, seemingly well off and relatively unstressed by work; our attraction to the show comes from a far more basic source: the strength of their friendships.

London has been influenced by a club set up by a group of Christians who wanted to do things differently. Steve Baker, the facilitator behind London club Abundant, explains that it's not about scalps on the convert board but about providing a quality healthy atmosphere for people to have fun, and a non-threatening environment for Christians to bring their friends.

Looking at the cult of shopping can also shed light on the phenomenon of the way people interact, or don't. Go out on your own for the day and make your purchases, and I'll challenge you to see how many shop assistants actually look you in the eye. My guess is that it will not be very many. This often strikes me as being slightly awkward; there I am, fully signed up to the blueprint interactions of this café culture, and I get treated like a plastic credit card holder. The lack of human contact is bizarre, and betrays the struggle within us between the pressures of an increasingly competitive job market – where slackers don't last long – and our desire to be treated as humans.

For example, consider how you might ask someone how their job is going. Instead of saying 'Is it fulfilling?' or 'Are you finding it fun?' we tend to opt for the classic 'Are you busy?' If we can't qualify our life as busy, people get worried if we are OK. It seems to me that to describe life or our work as 'busy' is a pretty sad description of things. Too often we fall into the trap of going along with the pressures that none of us like to face. This has been brought home to me of late, and I have tried really hard to avoid asking and answering in such terms. After all, I don't want my work life to be measured in terms of busyness – I'd much rather opt for purposefulness and satisfaction.

It always strikes me that any look at Jesus will come back with – among others – the conclusion that he was a man well stocked up on time and compassion. Although Jesus was extremely focused on what his life and three years of travelling work was about, he was always inter-ruptable and took time to be with people on his journey. Luke 18 tells a great story of Jesus meeting a blind beggar. This happens when he is on the way to Jericho, passing through a small village. As usual there's a crowd that quickly gathers round him, and out of it cries the beggar, 'Son of God, have mercy on me!' He receives nothing more than instructions on how to shut up from the crowd, so he cries out again. This time Jesus approaches him and asks him how he can help him. Not surprisingly the beggar mentions that he wouldn't mind being able to see again, and Jesus – cryptic and unusual as ever – tells him to clear off as his faith has made him see, which it has.

It amazes me that there are so many other stories of a similar nature, where Jesus puts pressure on his schedule by preferring to spend time with people in need. It's frighteningly easy for us to ignore his example, getting wrapped up in our own 'busy' schedules. I've tried hard not to do this, but it is difficult: the pressures soon mount up, and telling your boss that you don't plan on working late as you've got some old friends to phone doesn't always go down too well.

I heard a story once about an out-of-town lady from New York who spent days on end cruising round highly polished department stores pursuing her hobby: window-shopping. In order not to get branded a frugal window-shopper, the lady carried with her a large bag from the plushest of stores, filled up with tissue paper. This gave her the camouflage she needed, and she looked to anyone watching just like all the rest of the successful, extravagant shoppers.

One day she was thumbing her way through the latest range of Versace pants when she saw another impostor arrive in the floor. This lady's camo was not nearly as good, and within seconds the whole floor had noticed the homeless woman shuffling down the aisles. Polite shoppers made lengthy detours to avoid being contaminated by her proximity, and the window-shopper was sure it would not take long before security came to resolve the 'situation'. It was with amazement then, that she watched as one of the assistants approached the vagrant, asked her what she wanted to try on and proceeded to spend the next twenty minutes bringing her alternative garments to consider. Eventually the homeless lady announced – drawing no surprise from the scornful window-shopper – that she wasn't going to make a purchase on this occasion. When the lady left empty-handed, our window-shopper heard the assistant say as she handed over her business card that if ever she wanted to come back and try some more on, she should ask for her by name and she would be glad to help. As the assistant went on with her tasks, the window-shopper noticed a badge on her lapel, bearing the letters WWJD.

Finding out and copying what Jesus would do in a certain situation makes a solid foundation for any relationship, and making the effort is well worth it. It is also not that hard, nor is it to be restricted to those chunky friendships that have been in place for years. All around you – from the bar person to the shop assistant, the *Big Issue* seller to the people on the train – there are people waiting to be cared for. Get on with it.

Reading about disgraced Tory Jonathan Aitken, I was intrigued to find out that the bailiffs had been sent in to recover anything that he had of value to pay his debts. They even took his Rolex, swapping it for a £3 digital from the local garage. He was dragged through the tabloids and had his life turned over. I know he messed up, but it all seemed rather harsh, so I wrote him a card to express some care. Now, I know that he's got better things to do, but within a week I got a letter back saying how much he appreciated the card. I was at first surprised, but then felt sad as I thought of many other people out there who are so in need of compassion and love that even the most simple of things makes a difference.

Nick Hornby's book *About a Boy* insightfully tells the story of a schoolboy named Marcus whose life is not going so well, particularly with his divorced mother trying to top herself. Will, a thirty-something who doesn't need to work, entertains himself with his fetish for dating single mothers. The story follows their meeting and the subsequent friendship, and the way they influence each other's lives for the better. Like them, we are all at our best when we are in relationships that are healthy and supportive.

I'm sure that this is what Jesus would do: as his publicists and agents would try and lead him from place to place, I imagine that he would go wandering off like he did in the temple as a boy, talking with people wherever he found them. What's more, the Bible makes it absolutely clear that Jesus was a master of relationships. Just look at his network of friends: John (the beloved disciple with whom he had a special relationship), Peter and James – who, along with John, were the ones that he confided in and took to special places. There were the rest of the twelve who he called, built together and empowered. As they grew, he began to send them out in pairs. They did what they had seen him do, and eventually each of the six pairs passed what they had learned on to another set of twelve. How do we know this? The next time that we read about Jesus sending people out is when he sends out the seventy-two, which is what happens when you multiply six pairs by twelve.

Not only did Jesus touch the lives of the disciples, but he also changed forever the lives of thousands of people whom he met along the way. These were the people who had experienced at first hand his words, his actions and his demonstrations of God's power.

Whoever we are, we all have the same basic need for an emotionally supportive relationship to be well rooted in our lives. It may be a spouse – the person with whom the Bible says that we are to become one flesh and one mind having left our fathers and mothers. As a single guy I can certainly say that not having such a relationship does not mean I am robbed of intimacy and support. But being single, as I am, I'm aware that my opinion of my marital status can change from week to week. If things are going well, then I absolutely love the freedom of not being attached, but if I'm not having a good time, then it can seem like an oppressive weight on my shoulders that makes any happiness hard to enjoy. At these times I feel the enticing pull of having someone around with whom I could share all the good and not-so-good things in my life. At the same time I know that being single does not strike my name from the list of those having meaningful and supportive relationships, as I am fortunate to have some really great friends.

Being a leader can often be a very lonely way of life; pioneering, breaking new ground and living slightly ahead of the people you're trying to serve means that there may not be a whole load of people around you. At the end of the day – like everyone – the leaders have to shoulder the responsibility for the pursuit of their dreams. The trouble is that often those dreams bring with them plenty of conflict. Being single can allow the leader to invest much more of themselves into their work, but it can provide a double dose of isolation and loneliness which makes intimate and supportive friendships vitally important.

If there is one friendship that I am particularly grateful that God has given me, it's with Steve. He is one of the leaders of the church I belong to and we meet every month or so. I'm a very driven person, always having new ideas about breaking out to achieve for the King and the kingdom in my lifetime. However, when I go and see Steve his focus isn't what I've achieved recently. Instead he looks out for me as a person, encouraging me to pursue God as well as other healthy relationships in my life. We chat about anything and everything, and I continually give Steve permission to keep me to account for living an authentic lifestyle.

There are a few other friends around who I can lean on, share things with, celebrate and cry with. These I call Jonathan relationships, taking their cue from King Saul's son (Jonathan) who was close to David, Saul's eventual successor. So good was their relationship that Saul became jealous of it, even trying to divide them. Later, the importance of such relationships is emphasised when David stays behind instead of going off to fight with the rest of the men. Without the support of Jonathan's friendship, David's defences were too low when he found himself in a difficult position, perving at Bathsheba as she took a bath in the open air. Had he not committed that first sin of staying back while the rest went into battle, the following pages would make for very different reading.

Thankfully Jesus modelled for us exactly what friendship means. John recorded Jesus's words as this: 'Greater love has no one than this: than he is willing to lay down his life for his friends.'

Sacrifice – even to the point of death – is the ultimate mark of friendship. We may not have to face up to it on a daily basis, but the situation can suddenly appear from round the corner, as it did to two young men I read about in the paper the other day. They were out driving – one of them having just passed his test – pushing it to the limit down some country lanes. The driver lost control over a hump-backed bridge, the car flipped and ended up in the canal. The passenger managed to get out of the car that was almost totally submerged, but once he was on the surface, he realised that his friend was still down below. He was trapped inside – unable to open the door – so for the next six minutes the passenger took deep breaths, swam down to his friend and breathed air into his mouth, keeping him alive until a passing trucker stopped and managed to open the door with a piece of scaffolding. Friends are so important to us.

The Human Hive

We live in the age of the networker, an age which can be summed up by the perspective on life that we are only ever one person away from the person that we need to talk to. When this book was almost formed in my head, I was starting to look around for a publisher. Having mentioned this to my friend Mike, he phoned up his editor and made an introduction for me and here we are – only one person away from the person I needed to talk to.

My friend Paul is a business consultant. His entire company works on the basis of networking, both formal and informal. Each employee has their CV held on a central database, listing their particular skills and experience. Whenever the company gets a new contract, the project manager will network around the company to build a team of people with the expertise required to complete the contract. The database will be one place to look, but more fruitful than that is often the personal relationships within the office itself. Through the continual interaction each employee has with their colleagues, the workforce gets to know the corporate strengths on offer through the individuals. And when Paul finishes a project, he doesn't get another one dumped on his desk straight away, but he has the responsibility to go out and network with the rest of the staff in order to help place his skills as best he can. People's motivation is helped by an annual bonus, based on performance.

There are two sorts of party people. Some arrive at a party where they know no one and immediately try to find one person with whom they can chat all night. Others will turn up and thrive on the opportunity of introducing themselves to a roomful of new people. I'm more of the second person myself, and relish the opportunity of leaving the party with a back pocket stuffed full of new business cards and scribbled phone numbers, ready for some more contact and excited about the potential our meeting represents. If you're this second type, you will find networking really easy, but if you're more like the first, it may be more difficult, but by no means is it impossible.

While I'm praying for my friends, I think of Jill Garrett who is the managing director of the Gallup Organisation in the UK. By working with some progressive companies and organisations, she and her colleagues meet some interesting and influential people. One of the questions Gallup poses in their leadership interviews is this: 'Describe your constituency.' One leader gave the response along the following lines: 'I know people from the Prime Minister to the *Big Issue* vendor round the corner from the office. In knowing the Prime Minister I can help people like the *Big Issue* vendor.'

Practically speaking, I suppose I follow a few basic principles whenever I meet someone. Initially I try to establish a point of contact, something that we have in common. It may be a line of work, a hobby, a holiday, person or hope. Whoever I meet I'm looking for a connection that will spark off a conversation and get us under way. Second, I'll look out for a reason to talk again at a later date, to see what the plan might be that God could hatch through the meeting. Third, when I'm networking I always make sure that I've got loads of my own business cards in my wallet. At every opportunity to extend the meeting into the future I'll offer my card. Finally, I always follow things through. If they are people that I want to keep in touch with I will always send them a letter, note or an e-mail within the week. I figure that this secondary contact burns you deeper in their memory and establishes a line of communication that can then go both ways at a later date.

Personally I'm a real e-mail boy. I flick open my PDA (personal digital assistant) anywhere that I've got five minutes and write e-mails to friends and contacts. Then out comes my mobile telephone with built-in modem and the PDA and mobile talk away as my e-mails are surfed across the Internet. I even edited this book on my PDA.

It can often take some time to realise the significance of a connection that you have made with somebody. In 1998 we sent the Joshua Generation newsletter to an organisation in America which has a similar vision to train and mentor new leaders. Their vice-pres Steve ended up making a couple of trips over here in the year that followed, and we spent time looking at ways of working together in the future. Things still aren't clear, but I believe that God has a purpose in the relationship that we have together and that, given time, good things will flourish, particularly as I make a visit to them.

I believe in prophetic relationships: relationships where you invest in what is to come, sowing where you want to reap. It's about making an effort to look towards the future that you think that God has in store for you, and building relationships in that direction, which may in time help that process along.

I was recently having a drink with an MP friend who is in the Shadow Cabinet who was telling me how a cross-party Christian group that he is part of is developing. It strikes me that the cell he belongs to is a prophetic statement of the co-operation that can exist cross-party. Even though their approaches and methods may be different, the mutual support that they offer each other helps them to work towards the common goal of serving their constituencies and working to make England a better country. What's more, they are a model to the rest of Parliament; that co-operation is both attainable and more valuable than back-stabbing and fighting.

I believe that the friendships that we have are there for a purpose; God has intended that we consider them to be functional and fully operational. Whether it is in our work life, our church life, our family life or our social life, we can use the relationships we've got for the benefit of all around us, and for the discovery of the life that we were created to live. Being a Christian means that in relating to our communities we can express the love and forgiveness of God himself.

This is the age of the relater; the person whose life is going to make a difference will be the person who can relate to others — a person who has friendships of intimacy and influence in the lives that they live.

Action

1 What are your most intimate relationships? Pray and thank God for the people he has placed you in relationship with.

2 Who are the significant people that God has given you in your work at this time? Write their names down and pray for them on a regular basis. I have a photo album of people who are important for me which is a great prayer prompt.

3 Make contact with that person you met recently at a party or meeting with whom there could be a significant working relationship.

Conclusion

Herman Cortez was an ambitious man. He was a professional soldier with aspirations way beyond his present experience. Growing up in rural Spain, he saw Columbus return from his discovery of America in 1492, marching through his home town of Estremadura en route to pay tribute to the king. As he watched the procession of exotic Native American Indians and fabulous riches, young Cortez made plans of his own.

Years later, stationed with the occupying force in Cuba, he was picked to lead a fact-finding mission to Mexico with the main aim of verifying reports of the country being home to an incredibly wealthy civilisation. At the last minute the then-governor of Cuba, Diego Velásquez, changed his mind. He decided that Cortez wasn't capable of leading such a major expedition and ordered him to stay behind. Missing out on the adventure was the last thing on his mind, and our ambitious little friend wasn't going to let anything as insignificant as a direct order stand in the way of his dream. In February 1519 he set sail from Cuba, landing on the coast near modern-day Veracruz on 21 April with 11 ships, 550 men and 16 horses.

He soon gained political control of the city. Once firmly entrenched in power, he renounced the authority of Velásquez and declared himself to be in supreme command. Bold and ambitious, but yet politically aware, Cortez sent a letter to King Charles I of Spain (also known as the Holy Roman Emperor Charles V). In this letter, he proclaimed himself to be a Christian ambassador to the heathen cultures of Mexico, and attempted to prove that he was correct to defy the authority of Velásquez. It wasn't only the King that he had to win round though, as widespread unhappiness and unrest among his forces threatened to undermine everything he had worked for. In an act that surely goes down as one of the most radical and extreme in history, Cortez burned the ships in which he and his fellow-Spaniards had arrived. There was no turning back; conquest was the only means of long-term survival.

If only the story could stop there. Cortez went on to reveal his dark side by slaughtering millions of Aztecs. Within a handful of decades his lust for wealth and power had wiped out the entire civilisation, as the population fell from an estimated twenty-five million at the time of conquest to a little over one million by 1605.

Cortez was a pitiful man; evil at the same time as being insecure about his abilities. He ruled by the sword but died a broken and pathetic individual in 1547. Those of us today who are brash and adventurous might share some of the better qualities of the man who left Europe for unknown lands, to discover unknown riches. Hernando Cortez was one of those defiant young idealists who cast their fate to the new world. In burning his ships his determination became his situation and there could be no way on other than forward. But Cortez wasn't the only one who signed up for a one-way ticket.

Therefore, since we are surrounded by such a great cloud of witnesses, let us throw off everything that hinders and the sin that so easily entangles, and let us run with perseverance the race marked out for us. Let us fix our eyes on Jesus, the author and perfector of our faith, who for the joy set before him endured the cross, scorning its shame, and sat down at the right hand of the throne of God. (Hebrews 12:1–2)

In my own way I suppose I burnt my boats in 1997. I moved to London and worked as an assistant evangelist with a growing organisation. It offered a regular, secure wage and plenty of opportunities to be involved in successful national and international trips. But then there was Joshua Generation; something I'd had the initial idea for in 1995. I knew it had the potential to be a lot more than just a hobby, but pursuing it as my job would mean living by faith with no guaranteed income of any sort and would be generally rather risky. The choice was between the guaranteed and the unknown, the certain and the risky, the comfortable and the dream. I burned my boats and headed on towards zero money, the feeling of being alone and the privilege of seeing God make something out of nothing. I'm heading further on and further in towards a stirring within this generation for God, to see a generation emerging that can build his kingdom in the world. Joshua Generation remains risky, but who said destiny was ever easy?

Your destiny lies in just one direction. The question is this: will you burn your escape routes? Will you make clear your determination to keep going forward? Will you run from damaging appetites? Will you shake off the sin which is in danger of consuming you? Will you chase and pursue your God? Will you discover the life you were created to live?

Joshua Generation is a team of people who partner local churches and organisations to help them envision, equip and empower a new generation for the church and marketplace. Current research shows that the UK church is in need of expertise and resources to reach and train young adults to live a life of destiny for Jesus Christ. The vision of Joshua Generation is to help churches in their work amongst the teens, twenties and thirties generations. We are committed to training and mentoring a new generation of leaders.

For further information or to ask one of the team to visit your local church please contact:

Joshua Generation
The Church Worple Road
Wimbledon
London SW19 4JZ
United Kingdom
Tel: 0208 947 1313
Fax: 0208 947 9414
Email: admin@joshgen.org
Web: www.joshgen.org

Andy Hawthorne

Mad for Jesus

The Vision of the World Wide Message Tribe

This is the story of one man's dramatic conversion and the blossoming of an ever-growing group of Christians set to take Christ into the most demanding and tough urban areas.

This huge vision has spawned a number of different related initiatives: we read about the exciting beginnings and the growth of the band, the World Wide Message Tribe, and about Cameron Dante's conversion and the stories of other members of the band. Just as powerful are the personal accounts of young Christians who, as part of the Eden project, have moved in to live in the city's devastated areas to encourage a sense of community. 2000 will see the Tribe link up with Soul Survivor for one of the greatest evangelistic rallies of all time, The Message 2000 – the climax of the biggest year of outreach to young people ever.

Andy Hawthorne was born in Manchester and rebelled as a teenager before being brought to Christ through his brother, Simon, a former punk rocker. He and Simon started a fashion business, and it was some of the tough youths that they employed that inspired them to organise The Message to Schools, the work of the World Wide Message Tribe, Eden and The Message 2000.

Hodder & Stoughton
ISBN 0 340 74563 0

Mike Pilavachi with Craig Borlase

For the Audience of One
The Soul Survivor Guide to Worship

Worship is great: the music, the dance . . . but isn't there more to it than that? Does God enjoy it as much as we do? What happens when the music stops?

Worship is not something we do for our own benefit. It is for God, the audience of one. We should be worshipping every minute of every day, and we don't need words or even a tune.

Soul Survivor is at the heart of the incredible revival in contemporary youth worship. FOR THE AUDIENCE OF ONE shows that, beneath the surface level of words and music, a phenomenal work of God – anointed, culturally relevant and biblically sound – is taking place, enabling people to be broken, healed and transformed by him.

This book should be read by everyone with a desire to go deeper in their worship, and includes a special section for worship leaders.

Mike Pilavachi is the founder of Soul Survivor and pastor of Soul Survivor, Watford, UK. Craig Borlase is a freelance writer and Press Officer for Furious? Records.

Hodder & Stoughton
ISBN 0 340 72190 1

Mike Pilavachi with Craig Borlase

Soul Survivor Life

The aim of the SOUL SURVIVOR LIFE serious is to explain the basics of Christianity and Christian living in down-to-earth, jargon-free language. The four books follow the pattern of life: birth, death, adolescence, mid-life crisis and death.

The first, WALKING WITH A STRANGER, explores what it really means to become a Christian, who God is and how we can build a personal relationship with him. MY FIRST TROUSERS looks at the challenges and rewards facing us when we start going deeper with Jesus. The Christian life is not easy, however, and WEEPING BEFORE AN EMPTY TOMB asks how to cope when the going gets tough. The final book, AFTERLIFE, is about facing the future, in particular death, heaven and eternity.

All published by Hodder & Stoughton

WALKING WITH A STRANGER: ISBN 0 340 73534 1
MY FIRST TROUSERS: ISBN 0 340 73535 X
WEEPING BEFORE AN EMPTY TOMB: ISBN 0 340 73536 8
AFTERLIFE: ISBN 0 340 73537 6

Sue Rinaldi

Trend

A Pattern of Life

Does history repeat itself? In search of a sacred space?
Who is Generation Y? Confused?
Does beauty come in all shapes and sizes?
Who are the modern icons?
Is shopping the new religion?
Obsessed? Is it really hip to be single?
Are men an endangered species?
Is girl power humiliating or liberating?
Distressed? Have you found what you are looking for?

In this ground-breaking and convention-shattering
book, Sue Rinaldi searches for the real agenda
behind the headlines and how current trends will
affect our future.

Sue Rinaldi has stormed Wembley Stadium with her music,
had her Christian beliefs grilled on the altar of BBC TV
and appeared in numerous media forums. An acclaimed and
outspoken singer/songwriter, she has released two solo
albums and five albums with chart-scoring band Heartbeat.

Hodder & Stoughton
ISBN 0 340 72215 0